THE CYGNET

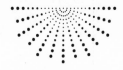

BRENDA HIATT

dolphin star
PRESS

The Cygnet
Hiatt Regency Classics #2

Copyright 1992 by Brenda Hiatt
Originally published as *The Ugly Duckling*
by Harlequin Books
Cover art by Fantasia Frog Designs

This is a work of fiction. Though some actual historical places, persons and events are depicted in this work, the primary characters and their stories are fictional. Any resemblance between those characters and actual persons, living or dead, are purely coincidental.

Dolphin Star Press

ISBN-13: 978-1-940618-62-3
ISBN-10: 1-940618-62-2

Dedication

For my parents, with love and gratitude

~

Other Hiatt Regency Classics

Gabriella
The Cygnet
Lord Dearborn's Destiny
Daring Deception
Christmas Promises (novella)
Christmas Bride
Azalea

CHAPTER ONE

"READ THAT LAST ONE AGAIN, DIDI! I VOW, IT IS ONE OF MY favourites!"

Deirdre smiled down at the golden head pillowed on her lap before repeating the sonnet she had just read. Then she stared out across the emerald lawns of the estate, shadowed at intervals by towering oaks like the one the two sisters rested beneath, quoting this time from memory:

"My love is strengthen'd,
    though more weak in seeming;
I love not less,
    though less the show appear;
That love is—"

"Here you are, Didi!" Lady Penrose interrupted her in exasperation. "I have been calling you these ten minutes past. Why did you not answer?"

"I... we did not hear you, Mama, did we, Faith?" replied Deirdre, looking to her younger sister for support.

"No, Mama," concurred Faith, quickly sitting up to dust bits of leaves and grass from her gown. "Didi was reading some of Shakespeare's sonnets to me, as I was feeling a bit poorly. And it did help! I feel ever so much better, now. When Didi reads poetry it is better than any medicine."

"Poetry, again!" sighed Lady Penrose, shaking her head in amused resignation. "I should have known. But, Didi, you must get your head out of the clouds and attend at once." Her voice became more severe. "Mrs. Chambers tells me that you did not appear for your fitting this morning. May I know why?"

Deirdre's pale cheeks pinkened slightly. "I…I must have forgotten. I took a walk after breakfast, and came upon some late crocuses two or three fields away, and—"

"And just had to stop to compose a verse about them," her mother finished drily. "Honestly, Didi! Was there ever such a girl for rhyming? I declare, I despair of you. Do you not realize that this is the third fitting you have missed? Celeste's wardrobe has been ready these two weeks and more, and yours is scarce begun. I'll not have you going to London looking like a dowd, I tell you to your head."

Lady Penrose gestured toward Deirdre's walking dress of thin grey wool, an old one which had once belonged to Althea, the eldest of Lord and Lady Penrose's six daughters. There was a sadly visible tear near the hem, and stains of grass and mud decorated the folds of the skirt.

"I wore this merely because I knew I should be sitting out

here with Faith, Mama," Deirdre said, attempting to defend herself. "Of course I do not intend to take this dress to London with me."

"I should say not!" Her mother was aghast at the very thought. "Your dowries may be spread thin among the six of you, but your father and I have at least the means to clothe our daughters properly for their debuts. But we cannot if you will not so much as go for your fittings! I have spoken to Mrs. Chambers, and she will expect you in one hour; so up you get, to put on something which will not shame the family, miss."

"Yes, ma'am," replied Deirdre, handing the volume of Shakespeare to Faith, who accepted it readily, and rising to follow Lady Penrose in the direction of the sprawling manor house. "But mightn't I forgo all of the frills and furbelows which Celeste has ordered for her gowns? It seems a shocking waste."

"Only because you care so little about your appearance," returned her mother. An active woman still possessing a fine figure, Lady Penrose set a brisk pace while privately admitting to herself that Deirdre was probably right. No amount of dressing would make her the beauty that Celeste —or the rest of her sisters, for that matter —was. Deirdre was decidedly the ugly duckling in a truly breathtaking flight of swans.

Not that Didi was truly ugly, her mama amended hastily to herself, nor even precisely plain. She only seemed so when set against her sisters' voluptuous, golden-haired beauty. Lady Penrose glanced sidelong at her fourth daughter, wondering for the hundredth time where Deirdre could have inherited that willow-wand slimness, or the fine, flyaway hair, so pale as to be almost white, which was now, as usual, twisted tightly into a bun at the nape of her neck. Mims, Lady Penrose's hairdresser, had long ago despaired of achieving even a remotely fashionable style with Deirdre's severely straight locks.

In addition to her physical appearance, Deirdre's attitude was completely at odds with that of her sisters or, indeed, any normal young lady soon to make her debut. A poet and dreamer, she had her head continually in the clouds and seemed unable to attend to such basics as fashion and etiquette for two minutes put together. Here in the country, "Dreamy Didi" managed well enough, but in London... In truth, Lady Penrose had little hope of firing her off creditably.

As if aware of her mother's thoughts, Deirdre said, "We may as well dress me simply and spend the money saved on Celeste. She pays for dressing and you know full well that I do not."

Stung by the truth of her daughter's words, as well as by the knowledge that the enterprising Celeste would whole-heartedly endorse such a plan, were she to hear of it, the Baroness quickly quashed the notion. "What you don't spend here you may spend in London, Didi. On yourself. You will not wish to find yourself looking a country bumpkin among the fashionable ladies there, I am certain."

She was not certain of this at all, in fact, and Deirdre clearly feeling even less so, the subject was allowed to drop.

Not quite trusting her daughter to choose something suitable to wear to the village, Lady Penrose followed Deirdre to her chamber. "A simple day dress will be suitable for your fitting, my dear, so long as it is not stained or torn," she commented, watching Marie, lady's maid to her unmarried daughters, throw open the doors of the wardrobe in the corner.

"I hope I may oblige you, Mama," replied Deirdre mildly.

4

"It has been so long since I went into Roseton, I cannot be certain anything I have meets such stringent standards."

Lady Penrose frowned at such flippancy, but soon realized with some dismay that her daughter had spoken nothing but the truth. Examining gown after gown of the pitifully small store in the wardrobe, she discovered none which was precisely suitable for venturing off the grounds. In fact, every single gown Deirdre owned appeared to be a cast-off of one or another of her sisters.

"My dear, I had no idea your wardrobe had got into this state!" she exclaimed as Marie held up the fifth gown for her inspection. "Why did you not mention it to me before?"

Deirdre smiled vaguely and shrugged. "I never really noticed," she replied. "Is there nothing here which I can wear to my fitting?" Her tone was hopeful.

Lady Penrose turned her eyes heavenward before surveying the rest of the room. She remembered now why she so seldom entered it: books, papers and quills littered every surface, not leaving space on the dressing-table for even such necessary feminine accoutrements as a ribbon box or bottles of perfume. Really, she thought, it looked more like some scholar's study than an eighteen-year-old girl's bedchamber! She would have suspected her husband's influence had she not known how seldom he bestirred himself to so much as speak to his offspring.

"I suppose this pale blue will have to do," she sighed finally, bringing her attention back to the matter at hand. The garment's only offence was a tea stain on one elbow. "And we shall rectify the rest of the problem in short order. I shall send Celeste with you, as she has mentioned a few odds and ends she still requires for Town." She could trust Celeste to broadcast her needs immediately. Shaking her head in indulgent exasperation at this least demanding and therefore most (unintentionally) neglected of her daughters, Lady Penrose quitted the cluttered chamber.

~

"Oh, Didi! What think you of this lavender ribbon? Will it not go divinely with my new bonnet, the one with the lilacs?" Celeste held up the aforementioned bit of silk for her sister's inspection.

"It appears more orchid than lilac to me," returned Deirdre, after eyeing the ribbon critically. Though taking no pains with her own appearance, she had a keen eye for colour and line. She had often wished that her few talents extended to painting, but had reluctantly decided, after one or two appalling (to her) attempts on canvas, to limit her artistic endeavours to poetry.

"But it is the closest to lilac in the shop. No doubt it will do well enough," decided Celeste, who tended to mix and match the hues in her ensembles with a lavish hand, apparently on the theory that to be colourful was to be noticed. And not to be noticed was anathema to the sprightly Celeste, who thrived on being the focus of any gathering.

"Have you not enough ribbons and laces already?" asked Deirdre in some dismay, surveying the growing pile of "odds and ends" her sister had collected in the time it had taken her to be fitted for one simple day dress. Whatever could Celeste have in mind for that scarlet feathered thing?

"Oh, I suppose I can scrape by with what I have until we reach London," Celeste replied reluctantly. "In fact, I suppose

I'd better, or I'll not have enough left in my clothing allowance to buy all of the very latest styles when we get there. And I absolutely *must* be slap up to the nines! Mama did say that we were only to buy enough here to be presentable for our first week or so in London." She gave a small sigh. "But I do so love this lavender ribbon..."

"Suppose I buy it, then give it to you?" offered Deirdre impulsively. "I've barely touched my allowance, and can't imagine needing a quarter of it, even in London, where they say things are so expensive."

"Oh, *would* you, Didi?" Celeste embraced her sister, earning a reproving look from Mrs. Chambers, who was pinning a second day dress around Deirdre. "You are the best of sisters! In that case, may I have this green parasol, as well?"

Deirdre was pleased to find that Celeste considered herself enough in her debt after this that she did not press for an explanation when Deirdre insisted on stopping in at the village post office on the way home.

The next week was so filled with preparations for the coming journey to Town that Deirdre had almost no time to devote to her beloved poetry. She managed to take occasional refuge in needlework, at which she had become amazingly proficient after discovering some years ago that she could compose freely in her head while her hands were busily occupied. If Lady Penrose had ever suspected the reason behind her daughter's enthusiasm for embroidery and other stitchery, she gave no sign.

Deirdre was not particularly reluctant to spend her

required Season in London, though she knew that fine gowns and accessories would not be necessary to her purpose there. For Deirdre's grand plan in accompanying her mother and sister to Town was to obtain, at the legendary bookstores she had heard of, some of the more current volumes of poetry available and perhaps to meet, in the flesh, one or more of those geniuses whose work she had read, admired and analysed. She especially hoped to have a chance to tell Lord Byron what she thought of the second canto of *Childe Harold*, not all of it good, for she prided herself more highly on her abilities as a critic of poetry than as a writer of it.

She also cherished a secret hope, shared only with Faith, of having a small volume of her own poetry published. To that end, with her younger sister's encouragement, she had some weeks ago written to Mr. Leigh Hunt, proprietor of the *Examiner*, asking if he might be willing to look over a few of her pieces. He had responded in the affirmative in a friendly if somewhat condescending letter and she had sent ahead some sample sheets while in Roseton with Celeste earlier in the week. In her meagre luggage, along with the few simple gowns she was bringing to Town, Deirdre intended to smuggle along some hundred or so pages of her other poetry, already tied neatly with a jaunty red ribbon.

Celeste's excitement, as the great day drew near, knew no bounds. A Season in London represented the culmination of all of her dreams and she constantly imagined herself a reigning belle of the ton, flirting with assorted earls, marquises and dukes, much to the detriment of the bonnet she was currently employed in trimming.

Lady Penrose bustled importantly about, overseeing the final preparations for herself and the pair of daughters that were to make their come-outs this Season. She had done the same three years earlier, when Althea had been nineteen and Beata eighteen, as these two now were; and she would repeat the process in two more years, when Elise and Faith would be nineteen and seventeen, though Elise chafed at the delay, begging hard to be allowed to make her come-out this year instead.

"But Mama," she pleaded again the night before their departure, tears of frustration in her eyes, "Faith will make her debut at seventeen, so why may not I?"

"Two daughters in London at once is all I feel able to handle," Lady Penrose had returned calmly for the twentieth time that week. "I still remember clearly the nervous exhaustion I suffered by the end of Althea's and Beata's Season. I vow, I thought dear Mark would never come up to scratch! Sir Bruce was much less of a worry, for he was clearly besotted with Althea from the first week."

"Surely you don't expect Didi to cause you any trouble, though, Mama— she goes mainly as a companion to Celeste, does she not?" enquired Elise tactlessly, unwittingly strengthening her mother's opinion that she was not yet ready for Society. "So if I came, you would still only have to worry about marrying off two daughters."

"No more out of you, miss!" snapped Lady Penrose sharply, glancing anxiously at Deirdre, who sat embroidering Celeste's initials onto a handkerchief, apparently absorbed in her work. It did not suit her to have the situation so open as that, though in reality she held no more hope of Didi marrying well (or even at all) than did Elise.

"Perhaps in two years' time you will have learned some decorum," she continued to her outspoken daughter. "Now it's off to bed with you and Faith. We need not discuss this again."

Faith followed Deirdre about like a small, mournful shadow as the week progressed. "I wish you would not go," she whispered to her sister, her lovely blue eyes, so like Celeste's in shape and colour, but so much more expressive, filling again with tears.

"I shall be back in the summer, sweetheart," Deirdre assured her with a motherly embrace. "Only think of the stories I shall have to tell you of the poets I shall meet, and the lovely ladies!"

"And you will have your poems printed," added Faith, beginning to smile again. "They are ever so much better than anyone else's—even those by Shakespeare himself, I vow!"

"You flatter me outrageously, Faith," replied Deirdre with a laugh. "But if they truly do get published, I promise that you will be the very first one I shall tell." Leaving Faith, whom she had mothered since her bout with scarlet fever many years before, and to whom she had always been "my Didi," was the one true regret she had about spending the spring in London.

The only one who did not concern himself in the flurry of activity presaging this significant event was Lord Penrose. He was a scholar and a recluse, endlessly researching the intricacies of ancient Hebrew and Aramaic in his private study, which work was only interrupted for meals and sleep, now as always.

Lady Penrose had thus ever had a free hand in the running of the household and estate, and the only interest she could ever remember her husband taking in his offspring was at the birth of the eldest, when he insisted that she and any which followed her be named alphabetically, that he might not confuse them in later years. With this Lady Penrose had complied, and she often counted herself lucky in comparison with her contemporaries that her lord made so few demands upon her, never questioning her very capable decisions on matters large or small.

With a final burst of preparation and excitement, all was ready at last and early one morning the Baroness settled herself into the luxurious travelling carriage with Celeste and Deirdre, all of them waving goodbye out of the carriage windows to a weeping Faith and a pouting Elise. Even Lord Penrose had left his books to see them off, in order to give a final admonition to Deirdre, who was his favourite daughter (when he remembered that he had any at all), since she showed the greatest propensity for scholarship.

"Don't neglect your studies in that vulgar social whirl, my dear," he said in parting. "The development of your mind must be your foremost ambition."

Lady Penrose tut-tutted, Deirdre smiled and Celeste bounced with impatience as the coachman whipped up the horses at Lord Penrose's signal. The carriage picked up speed as it rolled down the long, smooth drive, followed by the smaller barouche carrying the servants and extra luggage they would need in the Capital. They were on their way, leaving the only life Deirdre and Celeste had ever known, for London and the girls' first Season.

CHAPTER TWO

LONDON WAS NOT QUITE WHAT EITHER OF THE SISTERS HAD expected. Deirdre had envisioned the metropolis as a teeming literary mecca, the city from which the likes of Blake, Byron and Lamb had sprung, wielding their pens as Athena did her sword. For her part, Celeste had volubly imagined streets thronged with elegant specimens of nobility, a place where one could scarcely venture out of doors without bumping into some duke or countess. The foggy grey reality which greeted them the morning after their arrival was somewhat sobering in contrast to such dreams.

Deirdre had been so tired upon their arrival at Penrose House the night before that she had formed no firm impressions of anything beyond her bed, but Celeste, who had slept for much of the trip, awakened her sister at first light, so excited was she to find herself at last in London.

"Didi, is it not famous?" she cried, flinging back the rose-coloured draperies surrounding Deirdre's four-poster to allow the wan light from the windows to fall upon her face. "We are well and truly here! Do you suppose Mama intends taking us round to the modistes this morning? I do hope so!"

Deirdre shielded her eyes with one hand, squinting up at her sister. "What time is it?" she asked groggily.

Celeste took no notice, but continued to chatter. "And we shall no doubt see Althea before the day is out, for she said in her last letter that she would be in London before us. I am certain she will have some grand entertainment already planned! Oh, how can you sleep on such a day?"

"Obviously, I can't," replied Deirdre, but she was smiling now. This Season meant so very much to Celeste, and Deirdre hoped that she would not be disappointed. "Let us go down and see if any breakfast is to be had."

Half an hour later they descended to the dining-room, clad, with Marie's help, in their best day dresses from the country. Deirdre looked about her with interest, for she had never visited Penrose House before, though she had heard much about it from her mother and two eldest sisters. It was built on different lines from Rose Manor, of course, being tall and narrow rather than rambling. It seemed nearly as large, however, with the family bedrooms on the second floor, the main drawing-rooms and a fair-sized ballroom on the first, and the dining-room, morning-room and another parlour on the ground floor. She assumed that the kitchens must be located somewhere below.

"Does not the house look fine?" asked Celeste, joining Deirdre in her inspection. "I do hope the ballroom will be large enough, though."

"It accommodated Althea's and Beata's balls, Celeste, so no doubt it will be equal to yours as well," said Lady Penrose, coming down behind them. She, too, was eager to get an early start on their first day in Town. The country was well enough, in its way, but one always felt so much more *alive* when one was in London, she thought.

Over a breakfast which indicated to the Baroness that the cook she had engaged sight unseen would need to be replaced, and quickly, Lady Penrose enlightened her daughters as to her plans for the day. "First, of course, we must call on Althea, who is already in Town. Beata, I believe, is not to arrive until next week."

"Beata is to be in London this Season?" broke in Deirdre eagerly. She and Beata had been close before her second-eldest daughter's marriage three years earlier, Lady Penrose recalled.

"Yes, Geoffrey is well over a year old now, and she seems willing to bring him along. I can scarcely wait to see my first grandson, I must admit, and begged her most shamelessly to come. And, of course, we shall see little Theodore this very morning!"

The aforementioned Theodore was Althea's son, born a month after Beata's, to his mother's chagrin. Althea, however, had not found it necessary to immure herself in the country last Season on the feeble grounds of possessing a new infant, as Beata had, and therefore had let no Town connections slip. Lady Penrose thus expected her eldest daughter to be of more use to their purposes than Beata might be. Also, she had ever found Althea's temperament, very like Celeste's, easier to understand than Beata's, who tended toward an ironic, double-edged wit which often left her mother and sisters at a loss.

"As you must know, the Season will not be fully underway for another week or two, and many of the best families will not have arrived yet," she continued.

"So there will be no ball, or rout, or levee, or... or anything tonight, Mama?" broke in Celeste mournfully.

"Certainly not, my dear. We came early so that I could get the two of you properly outfitted before the invitations begin to arrive. And levees do not occur in the evening, Celeste, kindly remember. Besides, there are your hairstyles to consider, a dancing master to engage and any number of other details to attend to before either of you will be properly ready to enter Society."

"Why, what is wrong with my hair? And I already know how to dance, Mama, as you know perfectly well. At the last ball in Bedford I never sat out once!" Celeste was clearly affronted at this implied criticism of her beauty and accomplishments.

"Yes, yes, darling, you dance well enough for our little country gatherings, but a London ball is another thing entirely. And poor Didi has never learned at all."

"Must I, ma'am?" Deirdre was startled. She had not thought of dancing as something which might be required of her in London, though of course she should have, she realized belatedly.

"Well, certainly you must!" exclaimed her mother and sister together.

"Think how it would look if you sat among the dowagers at every do," Lady Penrose suggested.

"Oh, yes, Didi, it would embarrass me to death!" added Celeste artlessly. Deirdre gave in reluctantly but gracefully and her mother continued elaborating on her plans for the day.

∽

Althea, now Lady Thumble by virtue of her marriage to Sir Bruce Thumble three Seasons ago, lived in an elegant three-storey town house on Clarges Street. It had not been quite so grand as Penrose House upon her marriage, but she had overseen extensive renovation and redecorating and turned it into quite a showcase. She had also managed, over the past three years, to become one of the ton's premier hostesses, and if some of the highest sticklers thought Lady Thumble sadly frivolous, they quickly admitted that her warmth and gaiety more than made up for it. She had become well known for her frequent entertainments, so lavish that they might have caused her husband to grumble at the expense, had he been less besotted with his lovely wife.

For lovely Althea remained. This was the first fact her mother noted when she and her daughters were ushered into her presence an hour later by her butler, a soberly clad individual whose dignified mien was belied by a friendly twinkle in his eye. Althea had never been able to bear dour servants, Lady Penrose recalled.

"Mama, I missed you so!" cried Lady Thumble, running to embrace her mother, and then her sisters. "It's been an age and more, I vow! And look at my little Celeste— why, you are every bit as beautiful as I was for my come-out."

"Yes, everyone at home has remarked on her resemblance to you, my dear," returned Lady Penrose complacently. She, too, had been a noted beauty in her youth and did not hesitate to take full credit for her daughters' looks— except for Deirdre, of course, who did not resemble her in the least. "But where is little Theodore? I am simply beside myself with impatience to see him, for he was still a mere babe two Christmases ago."

"Oh, yes, he has grown amazingly and is the cleverest thing

imaginable," replied Althea, ringing for the nurse. "He was saying 'mama' before he was a year old, if you will believe it!"

While waiting for this remarkable child to make his entrance, Althea, Lady Penrose and Celeste animatedly discussed the modistes to be visited that day. "For one look at your gown, dear Althea, proves that Mrs. Chambers is not nearly so *au courant* of the latest fashions as she would have us believe," declared the Baroness. "And of course we must fire off our Celeste in prime style."

Lady Thumble looked fondly on the young lady just mentioned; their similarity in looks was echoed by one of temperament which had encouraged a closeness between the two, continued by correspondence after Althea's marriage.

"Indeed we must, Mama," she agreed. "Which reminds me to tell you that I have already spoken to Sally Jersey about your vouchers for Almack's, though she tells me that you, ma'am, have never allowed your membership to lapse."

"Yes, it seemed worth the ten guineas, even though I come to Town so seldom, but I welcome your assistance for your sisters. Now, which— Ah, here is my little gentleman!" Lady Penrose broke off with a coo on the entrance of a chubby, golden-haired cherub. Seventeen-month-old Theodore claimed her complete attention, as well as that of his two fond aunts, for the remainder of the visit.

~

"And may I also have the lemon silk with the green net over-drape?" Celeste asked her mother eagerly a few hours later. She had already amassed a formidable selection of gowns, in the brightest colours her mother would allow for a debutante.

"I suppose so, sweetheart," her fond mama replied, exchanging indulgent smiles with Madame Jeannine, who was volubly delighted with every one of her extravagant young customer's choices. "Yellow is demure enough, though the green is rather vivid. What about this cherry ribbon to set off the white muslin?"

"Yes, Celeste, and this cherry-and-white parasol will be perfect with it," supplied Deirdre, picking up the article mentioned. She had stayed in the background for much of the shopping expedition, gazing rapturously about at all the novelties encountered, no doubt storing them up to put into future poems. The few suggestions she had made thus far, however, had been surprisingly good ones. Only now did the Baroness realize that her younger daughter had ordered but three gowns thus far.

"Honestly, Didi, one would think you were seeking a post as a governess, what with the choices you are making in gowns," Lady Penrose commented, looking over her selections.

While Celeste exclaimed over every brightly coloured silk, satin, lutestring and muslin which was paraded before them, begging earnestly to be allowed at least a few deeply coloured gowns, Deirdre refused to consider any but the plainest (and least expensive) styles. Pastels suited her, to be sure, with her pale colouring, but her mother feared she would fade into the wallpaper next to her more flamboyant sister. Lady Penrose was determined that Deirdre should have her fair chance at attracting an eligible mate, no matter how unlikely it seemed.

"Nonsense, Mama. A governess would scarcely wear peach silk, I think," replied Deirdre with a smile. "And I've told you a dozen times that frills and furbelows are wasted on me. Let

Celeste spend what I save, that she may better attract her duke. I'll be perfectly content with a humble viscount myself, who surely cannot expect the same degree of ornamentation in a wife."

Celeste giggled at Deirdre's silliness, but Lady Penrose frowned. "Making a suitable match is serious business, miss, and I'll thank you not to jest about it."

Deirdre said nothing, as she had no desire to enter into another argument with her mother about marriages of convenience. She had determined long ago that even abject poverty would never tempt her into anything but a love match, and she therefore cheerfully expected to go to her grave unwed. But in her poetic, romantic heart she hoped that Celeste might achieve what was out of her reach, and she intended to further that end in any way she could. The more beautiful Celeste was, she reasoned, the more swains she would have to choose from— which should increase the chance that she would fall in love with one of them. And if that one should happen to be a duke, why then, everyone would be happy.

When the ladies left the modiste's two hours later, Celeste having ordered three gowns for every one of Deirdre's, and having spent easily five times what her sister had, Deirdre felt with satisfaction that she had done what she could to further her sister's ultimate happiness. In fact, seeing Celeste swathed in Madame Jeannine's lovely fabrics had inspired a romantic sonnet she could hardly wait to write down when they returned to Penrose House.

Looking over the lines after she had penned them, Deirdre was sharply reminded of her promise to Faith— and to herself. She had done what she could to further Celeste's ambitions, she thought, adding the new sonnet to the collection of poetry she had brought along. It was now time to give some thought to her own.

"Marie, can you discover Mr. Leigh Hunt's direction?" Deirdre asked the abigail, who was bustling about her room, having finally finished the last of Celeste's unpacking. Deirdre had done her own last night, as it had taken no more than a few minutes to bestow the few things she had brought.

"I...I suppose so, Miss Didi. If young William doesn't know, he can find it out quickly enough. That lad seems up to anything and everything." She referred to the boy they had hired upon their arrival as stable-hand and errand boy, a bright, freckle-faced urchin of fourteen.

"Good. I'd like you to see that this is delivered to him, Marie— discreetly," said Deirdre, turning to retrieve her bundle of verses from the bottom drawer of her writing desk, where she had placed it the night before.

Marie took a step backward, frowning. "Miss Didi!" she said awfully. "Surely you can't be expecting me to deliver a personal letter from you to some gentleman! Whatever would your mother say?"

Deirdre was unable to suppress a giggle at Marie's expression, which only served to deepen the maid's suspicions. "Really, Marie! Does this look like a letter?" She held up the thick, ribbon-bound sheaf of papers. "Mr. Hunt, I'll have you know, is the proprietor of the *Examiner*, a literary newspaper. And this is a collection of some of my poetry, which he has asked to see. It is quite a wonderful opportunity for me, don't you think?"

Marie still looked doubtful, but she stopped frowning. "So it's to his newspaper office you want these took? I suppose that's not quite so bad."

"Yes, I should think you, or young William, can discover where the *Examiner* is published without asking any awkward questions of the other servants. I would really rather Mama and Celeste did not hear of this just yet." She was not sure whether their reaction would be one of amusement or horror, and was equally averse to either.

"Of course, Miss Didi, I understand," replied Marie unexpectedly. "You want to surprise them by showing off your poetry all printed up in the paper! 'Twill be a very good joke, and quite innocent, to my way of thinking." Marie also thought it might show her ladyship that Miss Didi would not stay in her sisters' shadows forever, which would be no bad thing, but she refrained from saying so aloud. She had always regarded Miss Didi's ability to write poetry, real poetry, with something akin to awe.

~

By the next morning the fog had dissipated, and the weather remained fair for the following week. Deirdre's spirits, at first brightened by the sunshine, gradually sank as she found herself trapped indoors by the incessant fittings, instructions in etiquette and dancing lessons. Her request that they might walk to the shops one day rather than ride in the closed carriage was met with horror from Lady Penrose, who informed her that only those without the means to maintain a carriage indulged in such vulgar exercise in Town, with the possible exception of in the Park.

"When you are both outfitted properly will be time enough for that, Didi," she declared, when her daughter quickly urged on her a sojourn in Hyde Park. "I'd prefer no one of importance saw you until you make your formal debuts at Althea's card-party on Tuesday."

"You mean I am not to have a ball?" wailed Celeste, over-hearing.

"Of course you shall, sweetheart," Lady Penrose quickly soothed her. "I only meant that Tuesday is to be your first public appearance in Society. We shall hold your ball in a few weeks, when everyone who matters is in Town."

"Oh." Celeste was mollified. "Will Didi have her own ball as well, or shall we both be presented at once?"

Lady Penrose glanced at Deirdre, considering. The expense of one ball would be extreme; two, while not actually beyond their reach, would stretch the resources she had budgeted for that Season to the utmost. She had managed one each for Althea and Beata, of course, but that had been different. Both of them had *wanted* to attach husbands.

As if reading her mind, Deirdre spoke before her mother could answer. "Two balls seems a shocking waste of money to me. Would it not be, Mama? I've no objection to being presented at Celeste's."

Lady Penrose smiled in relief, reflecting on how convenient it sometimes was that Didi was so easily satisfied. "It would be more economical, I'll allow," she conceded. The Baroness prided herself that her careful management had increased the family wealth over the years.

Celeste began at once to plan for the ball, not thinking to consult Deirdre on her preferences; nor did it occur to Deirdre that she should.

∾

When the hairdresser Lady Penrose had engaged made her appearance on Tuesday afternoon, the same pattern followed. Celeste had very particular ideas as to how she wanted her hair cut and arranged, and only found it to her satisfaction when it was nearly time to dress for the evening. There was no time by then for anything but the simplest cut for Deirdre's hair, but she declared that she did not mind in the least.

"If you can even up the ends it will suffice," she told the horrified Mrs. Jagels. "I generally just pull it back from my face in a tail or bun, anyway."

"Oh, but don't you want something special for Althea's do, Didi?" asked Celeste, perhaps feeling just the tiniest pang of guilt for having monopolized the woman's available time.

"Not especially," replied Deirdre with a smile. "At any rate, there's no time." Celeste had to concede the truth of this last statement, and went to dress without further argument.

Mrs. Jagels had to content herself with working Deirdre's fine, flyaway hair into a braid before coiling it into a knot at the nape of her neck. She, along with the new cook, had come on Marie's recommendation, and she had taken the abigail's advice in learning several bewitching styles which could be achieved with this baby-fine blond hair, but all of them required more time than was now available.

"We'll come up with something much nicer next time, miss, you'll see," she promised Deirdre as she took her leave.

Deirdre smiled and nodded, but rather doubted the woman's words. If Mims, who had been with the family for nearly ten years, had never produced anything better than a bun, she didn't see how Mrs. Jagels, who was seeing her hair for the first time today, possibly could. She had occasionally wished that she, too, might have been blessed with the thick curls which her sisters possessed in varying shades of rich gold, but had never allowed the lack of it to trouble her unduly. After all, what need had a poet of an alluring appearance? Anyone who would be attracted to her merely for the sake of external beauty was surely not worth knowing.

CHAPTER THREE

THE TERM "CARD-PARTY" HAD SUGGESTED TO BOTH CELESTE and Deirdre a small, informal gathering, but they found immediately upon their arrival at Lady Thumble's that they were far off the mark. The small ballroom had been set with numerous tables for four, as whist was to be the order of the evening, but many more people had obviously been invited than the card tables would accommodate. A lavish buffet was laid out in the supper-room adjoining the ballroom, with additional tables intended for the diners.

Althea, considering herself jointly responsible with the Baroness for launching Celeste successfully, had invited every eligible bachelor she could think of, as well as a few literary types for Deirdre's sake. As this was not to be a formal dinner-party, she cared not if the numbers came out evenly and there was a preponderance of gentlemen as a result.

"Mama, are not Althea's decorations lovely? And did you ever see such an elegant crowd?" exclaimed Celeste after nearly thirty seconds of unwonted speechlessness at the scene.

Indeed, Lady Thumble had outdone herself by having the tables laid with cloths of every colour of the rainbow. Paper flowers of similarly varied hues hung from hooks along the walls as well as from the sconces, and adorned each table so liberally as to almost certainly interfere with card-playing.

Deirdre thought the total effect rather overpowering, but could not be surprised that it met with her sister's approval, as Althea and Celeste shared a preference for vivid colours. Celeste herself looked like a princess from a fairy-tale in her sky-blue satin evening gown with a pink gauze overdrape. Flowers of brighter pink and blue were woven through her gleaming gold tresses, which were piled intricately on top of her head, save for a cloud of ringlets arranged artfully about her winsome face.

Deirdre, on the other hand, bore an unfortunate resemblance to an upper servant in her plain, silver-grey gown ornamented only by narrow ruffles of silver lace at wrists and hem, at least according to their mother. But the contrast between her sister's attire and her own bothered her not at all. She looked about eagerly at the gathering guests, wondering if Lord Byron might have been invited.

"Oh, Althea, everything is simply beautiful!" cried Celeste as their hostess approached to greet them. "And I'm simply *dying* to meet some of the gentlemen —and ladies, too, of course," she added quickly, catching her mother's frown. "We have been introduced to no one in Town thus far and I am like to die of loneliness!"

Althea gave her a quick hug, with a smile for Deirdre and their mother. "Well, we certainly cannot have that, sweetheart. That is why I made sure to invite so many eligible *partis*. Now, Lord Linley over there is merely a viscount, but wealthier than many more highly titled gentlemen, and he has already expressed a desire to meet you. Fear not, though, for I also intend to bring you to the attention of a duke or two...."

She and Celeste went off arm in arm to meet the gentlemen, Lady Penrose and Deirdre following more slowly. "I vow, Althea has not changed a bit, and Celeste is so very like her," the Baroness murmured, smiling fondly after them. "Come, Didi, I shall introduce you to Lady Heatherton, who was my dearest friend some years ago. I believe she has a daughter your age making her come-out this Season, as well."

It was a successful evening all round. Lady Thumble had the satisfaction of knowing that her card-party would be described as the first crush of the Season, graced as it was by nearly every political, literary and fashionable person of note already residing in the Capital. Lady Penrose had the pleasure of renewing several acquaintances, as well as that of seeing her darling Celeste surrounded by eligible young men like a flame by moths.

Deirdre was equally pleased to see Celeste so universally admired, and had the added thrill of making the acquaintance of Mr. Walter Scott, who listened with apparent delight to her comments on *The Vision of Don Roderick* and *Rokeby*, and of Robert Southey, whose poetry she found unpleasantly macabre, but whose style she admired. He was an intimate of Samuel Coleridge and William Wordsworth, neither of whom were in London just then, and he mentioned their names with a casualness which Deirdre could only envy. What must it be like, she wondered wistfully, to live always in such circles, communing with such great minds as an equal?

"You have a keen talent for critique," commented Southey after she had mentioned what she considered the high and low points of his *The Curse of Kehama*. "Do you write poetry as well?"

"I... ah, yes. Yes I do, though of course it is nothing to—" She broke off, becoming aware that Althea was at her elbow, introducing another gentleman to her, a tall young man with a thin, clever-looking face and an astonishing pink-and-gold waistcoat.

"Didi, my dear, this is the Honourable Jonas Flinder, son of Lord Mallencroft. I mentioned in his hearing that you dabbled in poetry and he immediately insisted upon meeting you. Mr. Flinder, my sister, Miss Deirdre Wheaton."

Deirdre began automatically to say what was proper, but Mr. Flinder interrupted by seizing her hand without warning and exclaiming, "Have I at last found a lady who can appreciate the finer points of the highest art yet attained by man? How fortunate for us both that we have found each other! Pray let me hear one of your offerings to the Muse, Miss Wheaton!" Althea giggled uncertainly as Deirdre gently withdrew her hand, saying, "I am sorry, sir, but I never recite my own poetry. I much prefer speaking aloud that of others, my particular preference being the sonnets of William Shakespeare. Whose work do you most admire, Mr. Flinder?"

This effort to put the conversation on a more conventional footing was successful and Althea left them deep in a discussion of the relative merits of Milton, Spenser and Dryden, feeling very pleased with herself.

"Mama," she whispered to Lady Penrose a few minutes later, "I believe I have discovered just the man for little Didi. Look over there." She indicated the corner table where Deirdre and Mr. Flinder had retired to continue their conversation.

"Who is he, my dear?" asked the Baroness with a lift of her brows.

Althea told her, adding, "He is only a second, or perhaps third, son, to be sure, but I'm told his income is tolerable, and will increase somewhat upon his father's demise."

Lady Penrose nodded her approval. Having Deirdre so easily settled would make the Season vastly more enjoyable for her, allowing her to concentrate all her energies on seeing that Celeste made the best possible match. Judging by her success tonight, her fond mama had begun to believe that even a duke might not be beyond her reach.

With all so agreeably occupied, the evening passed swiftly for Lady Penrose and her daughters. Deirdre quite forgot her disappointment at Lord Byron's absence in the pleasure of the various literary acquaintances she had made. It was a thrill, hitherto unknown in her experience, to be included in their conversations and to have her opinions listened to as attentively as if she were an equal. Her discussion with Mr. Flinder was enjoyable as well, if not on so high a plane.

It must have been near eleven when Deirdre looked up from the card-table where she was playing a hand of whist with Julia Heatherton, Mr. Flinder and a Mr. Miller, to see a gentleman who had apparently just that moment arrived. As he stood surveying the crowd from the far side of the room, Deirdre felt her heart give a sudden, unsettling thump.

He was handsome, to be sure, with carelessly arranged dark hair and chiselled features, his athletic frame easily topping six feet; but there were any number of handsome gentlemen present tonight, none of whom had affected Deirdre in the least. It was not merely his face and figure, fine as they were, which caused Deirdre to misplay her hand, eliciting a crow of triumph from Miss Heatherton at her easy victory. There was something about him which seemed to call out to her, irresistibly drawing her attention. The man turned his head slightly and Deirdre felt as if an invisible hand squeezed her heart within her.

"Excuse me," she said absently, rising abruptly from the table, to her companions' surprise. "I must speak with my sister."

As if in a daze, still uncertain what was possessing her, Deirdre sought out Lady Thumble, who was giving one of the servants instructions regarding the lobster patties. "Althea?" she murmured as soon as her sister had finished speaking. "Who is that man? No, the one over there, by the door."

Lady Thumble turned to look. "He is come after all!" she exclaimed in obvious delight. "That is the Marquis of Wrotham, Didi, without a doubt the most sought-after bachelor in London these several Seasons past. I had not heard that he was in Town yet, though I sent him an invitation just in case. His being here is quite a coup for me, for he is extremely selective about the entertainments he attends. I must count myself lucky, I suppose, that nothing else of importance is taking place tonight."

At another time, Deirdre might have remarked that the gentleman's late appearance showed a lack of regard for his hostess, but just now she was too distracted to think of it. Having read of the symptoms in hundreds, nay, thousands of love sonnets over the years (not to mention a few that she herself had written), Deirdre was beginning to realize what had befallen her: she had been smitten by that cherubic archer himself, Cupid. The shaft had struck with all the force and

unexpectedness the little deity was famous for, and undoubtedly would be as impossible to extract.

"... Is Celeste?" Althea was saying. "I must try to introduce
her to his notice, though I can't in honesty expect that much
will come of it. He has shown himself incredibly adept at
avoiding parson's mousetrap thus far." If Deirdre had been
attending, she might have suspected from her sister's
aggrieved tone that Althea had been one of the ladies so disappointed.

Just then Lady Penrose came hurrying up, Celeste in tow.
"Althea, you sly thing! You said nothing about Wrotham being
here tonight!"

"Indeed, Mama, I thought he was still abroad," replied
Lady Thumble, clearly still in a high state of excitement. "I
must go greet him, of course. Celeste, if you would care for an
introduction, I suggest that you accompany me."

Deirdre hung back as her sisters and mother swept across
to where the Marquis of Wrotham stood conversing with two
other gentlemen. She was fully conscious, perhaps for the first
time, of how drab and, well, *mousy* she looked compared to
Celeste. And much of it her own doing! This was not the first
impression she wanted to create in this man who affected her
so profoundly. Besides, she realized, no one had so much as
mentioned introducing her to him.

She watched, from her position near the buffet tables, as he
inclined his noble head, first to Althea and then to the
Baroness, before taking Celeste's hand and bowing over it.
Deirdre was vaguely relieved that he did not actually kiss it, as
many of the other gentlemen had done. She could detect no
particular warmth in his expression as he looked at Celeste,

though she admitted to herself that she was likely seeing only what she wished to.

He turned away soon to speak to others about the room, and Deirdre watched him closely, willing herself in vain to see him as no different from any other distinguished, handsome gentleman in the house. It was no use. The more she tried to convince herself that she was merely tired, or that he simply reminded her of someone she had once known, the more certain she became that she was in the grip of the poets' most exalted emotion.

I shall simply ignore it, she told herself finally. *There are such things as fleeting passions, as well as lasting ones. Perhaps this is one of the former; indeed, it must be, for I don't even know the man. Surely it is not possible to form a true attachment to someone without so much as speaking to him!*

Having resolved this, Deirdre sought out Miss Heatherton again. Although she had discovered her to be a frivolous, insipid girl, in whose company she found no particular delight, she also suspected that she was not particularly bright, and perceptiveness was one thing Deirdre wished to avoid until she had herself completely in hand.

"Shall we finish our rubber now, Didi?" asked Julia as she came up. Deirdre winced, wishing fleetingly that her mother had not introduced her by the family nickname, but assented readily.

"Let us try to find our partners again," she suggested. During the search, Julia chattered cheerfully about last Season's scandals, the present one being too new to have yet generated any gossip worthy of note. Deirdre felt her emotions settling as she listened to the other girl's prattle; what she had felt before had doubtless been a simple affliction of the nerves, she decided.

Catching another glimpse of Lord Wrotham as they attempted to locate Mr. Miller, however, she was dismayed to find her pulse behaving much as it had at her first sight of him. Firmly, she looked away, determined to control such unseemly emotion.

They had scarcely begun to play again when Lady Penrose motioned Deirdre to her side to inform her that they would be leaving shortly. Looking around, Deirdre realized that the company had thinned noticeably already.

"Well, we're sure to see each other about, Didi," said Julia brightly. "I shall come to call one day soon, or you may come to see me. Good night!"

As the Penrose party took their leave, at least a dozen gentlemen begged Celeste's permission to call on her the next day, and she took her time deciding which one most merited the privilege of taking her out driving in the Park the day following that. She finally settled on Sir Malcolm Digby— only a baronet, but easily the handsomest of the lot. Lord Wrotham, Deirdre noticed, was not among the throng about her sister, having apparently left within an hour of his arrival.

Mr. Flinder hurried up at that moment. "Miss Wheaton!" he said urgently, "might I call on you tomorrow?"

Deirdre smiled her assent, glancing at her mother for confirmation. Lady Penrose obviously had no fault to find, smiling even more broadly than her daughter before turning back to Celeste and her throng of admirers.

"I...I have a favour to ask of you as well," he continued, suddenly appearing self-conscious.

"A favour?" Deirdre was intrigued.

"Might I...that is...would you mind looking over a bit of *my* poetry? I was much impressed by your insights on the masters of the art and would greatly value your opinion of my talents. If you would be so kind?"

Deirdre was flattered, but made haste to be honest. "Certainly, if you wish it, Mr. Flinder, but I warn you that I am apt to be frank in my criticism. I would not wish to risk offending you and thus losing a friend."

Mr. Flinder bowed. "I am deeply honoured to be numbered among your friends, Miss Wheaton. And I would never ask you to be anything but frank about my work. Pray, feel free to be as harsh as is necessary. If your criticism induces me to improve, I can only be indebted to you."

"In that case, Mr. Flinder, I would be pleased to see your work. I look forward to receiving you tomorrow." As she spoke, Deirdre was conscious of a fervent hope that Mr. Flinder's poetry might show more depth and intelligence than his analysis of the great poets had, for she would hate to offend one of the few friends she had made during her first week in London.

Throughout the carriage ride home, Lady Penrose happily reviewed the evening, totting up Celeste's noble conquests with relish. "I dare swear we should make up a list, ranking them from most to least desirable as husbands, my dear, if the idea were not so absurd," she tittered at one point, quite giddy with her daughter's success on her first evening out.

"Why would it be absurd, Mama?" asked Celeste practically. "It seems an excellent idea to me. I fear I shall have an impossible time choosing between them, else."

They chattered on in this vein for most of the way and Deirdre largely ignored them, as she was obviously not expected to take part in the discussion. Instead, she took the opportunity to relive the earlier part of the evening, when she had enjoyed conversations with so many literary luminaries—until she was abruptly jarred back to the present by the mention of Lord Wrotham's name.

"For he would undoubtedly have to go at the very top of the list, my dear," continued Lady Penrose playfully.

"He may be very wealthy, Mama, but I found him not nearly so pleasant as many of the other gentlemen I met tonight," returned Celeste, taking the game more seriously. "The man scarce spoke two words to me! Besides, did he not once raise Althea's hopes, only to dash them? I would not wish to be treated so, I vow!"

"Still, if the opportunity arises, you may as well be pleasant to him. There is no point at all whistling such a fortune down the wind, you know, and he is so highly placed in Society that it would never do to offend him," Lady Penrose cautioned quickly.

"Oh, I shall not be rude to him, Mama, but I shan't set my cap for him, either. Now what of Glovington? He is an actual duke, but you don't mention him."

"Because he is already married, miss! His duchess resides in the country...." Deirdre allowed her attention to wander again, though in a different direction.

Lady Penrose suddenly recalled her presence in the carriage as they pulled up to the steps of Penrose House.

"By the bye, Didi, you seemed to enjoy yourself as well," she said cheerfully. "But if you wish to attach young Mr. Flinder or any other of the gentlemen you met, you really must take more pains with your appearance."

"Perhaps I shall, Mama," she murmured thoughtfully. "Perhaps I shall."

Lady Penrose smiled knowingly at this evidence that Deirdre apparently returned Mr. Flinder's regard. How neatly things were working out, she thought, before returning her attention to the question of the relative eligibility of her other daughter's suitors as the footman opened the carriage door and let down the steps.

CHAPTER FOUR

THAT OF THE DOZEN OR SO GENTLEMEN WHO CAME TO CALL THE next morning, only one asked for Miss Deirdre Wheaton, surprised no one, least of all Deirdre herself. Celeste, upon descending to breakfast, was greeted with the welcome news that no fewer than fifteen bouquets of flowers had been delivered already, with more undoubtedly to follow.

"And I'm certain I don't know where I'm to put them all, miss," continued the aggrieved housekeeper. "Every level space in the drawing-room is already filled, and the morning-room, too."

"Oh, just put the overflow on the dining-room table," said Celeste blithely. "A leaf or two can always be added if it becomes necessary. Later, I shall select two or three of my favourites for my bedchamber, and Didi may have some for hers, as well," she added generously, with a smile for her sister.

It did not occur to Deirdre to be offended. "I was certain

you would be a great success, Celeste," she said warmly, returning the smile. "I just hope you will take the time to acquaint yourself with these gentlemen and not be swept away by the first one to make you an offer. Pray don't settle for a man who is merely wealthy or handsome, whom you cannot love."

Celeste giggled. "La, Didi, I have no mind to accept anyone yet, nor even in the next few weeks. I wish to thoroughly enjoy my first Season before tying myself to any one man!"

Deirdre had to content herself with that. She suspected that their mother might not be so patient, however, were one of the gentlemen at the top of her fictitious "list" to request Celeste's hand.

Lord Linley was the first of their callers, with Sir Malcolm Digby and Lord Naseby close on his heels. Deirdre soon lost track of the names and titles, though Celeste seemed to have no such trouble. In fact, Deirdre could only admire her sister's skill in somehow flirting simultaneously with all of them without raising either her mother's eyebrows or any particular admirer's hopes. She was smiling at her image of Celeste manipulating marionette strings attached to said suitors, when Mr. Flinder was announced.

"My dear Miss Wheaton," he exclaimed, coming to sit next to Deirdre with scarcely a glance at her lovely sister. "Dare I hope you have been longing as I have for a resumption of our sublime communion of last night?"

Celeste smiled briefly in his direction before turning her attention back to Mr. Gellings, who was relating a bit of gossip from the Little Season last autumn. She could not begrudge her sister Mr. Flinder's attention, as he was neither handsome enough nor rich enough to interest her, and did not even possess a title.

"Good morning, Mr. Flinder," responded Deirdre readily. "I, too, enjoyed our discussion of the poets."

"Please, Miss Wheaton, could you not find it in your heart to call me Jonas? I feel we have become great friends already, almost as though our minds are linked."

Deirdre smiled uncertainly, glancing over to where Lady Penrose sat discussing politics with Sir Malcolm, but her mother had obviously not heard. Deciding that it would be foolish to stand on ceremony with a fellow poet, however, she said after only the slightest hesitation, "Certainly, Jonas, and you must call me Didi, as my family does."

Jonas beamed upon her and launched immediately into what sounded suspiciously like a prepared speech. "Miss Wheaton, Didi, I could not help but notice last night that you seemed on very good terms with Mr. Southey, Mr. Scott and Mr. Peacock. I realize that a lady of Quality like yourself cannot take a serious interest in a literary career, but it is my highest aspiration to make my living as a poet; sleeping, eating and breathing in the heady aroma of the Muse's inspiration." He paused, regarding her hopefully, as if gauging her reaction thus far.

Deirdre saw no point in contradicting his assumptions about her interests— indeed, her thoughts had already wandered to Lord Wrotham, as they had with alarming frequency since last night, so that she scarcely knew what Jonas had said. She motioned for him to continue.

"To be perfectly honest, I have been trying for the past two years to become a part of the circle to which you, as a lady and sister to the eminent Lady Thumble, were so readily admitted last night. You have already called me your friend, Didi. As such, you could be of great help to me."

"How?" she asked curiously, her attention caught for the moment.

Jonas leaned forward, smiling, evidently taking her response as an agreement. "Read my poetry," he said eagerly, "and mention it to those exalted gentlemen at your next opportunity. They seemed last night to respect your opinions. Once they have an intimation of my promise as a poet, surely one of them will be willing to give me the patronage, the notice, that my career requires just now."

He reached down and lifted a packet of papers, very like the one Deirdre had sent off to Mr. Hunt, only rather thicker. She was struck immediately by the parallel and nearly blurted out where her work had been sent, but something held her back. If Mr. Flinder— Jonas— knew of that, might he not ask that she do likewise with his poetry? Deirdre had no intention of committing herself to such a course until she had opportunity to judge his work for herself.

"I...I'll do what I can, of course, Jonas. As a friend."

Jonas pressed her hand in gratitude. "Thank you, Didi. I am equally willing to look over any verses you may have written, if you wish."

"Perhaps later. But I wanted to ask if you have read the sonnet 'O Solitude' which appeared last month in the *Examiner*. It is the work of a new poet on the scene, John Keats, and I thought it showed promise of great talent." She hoped that, by keeping her thoughts on poetry, she could banish the disturbing feelings which continued to assail her.

After his requisite quarter of an hour had passed, Jonas took his leave, very pleased with the progress he had made with Miss Wheaton. It had occurred to him during the visit that if she could be of assistance to him as a friend, she might be of even more use as a wife. He would make discreet enquiries as to the size of her dowry. She was not especially ornamental, he had to admit, but intelligence and an appreciation for poetry— particularly his poetry— might well compensate for a lack of beauty. And there was always Drusilla over in Seven Dials, as lovely as she was stupid, to attend to his more carnal needs.

Sitting over needlework for the remainder of the morning as Celeste's callers came and went, Deirdre attempted to compose but found that she could not. Lord Wrotham's face kept haunting her, and she began to suspect that her first impression of what had befallen her was correct. She was in love, and with a man whose first name she did not even know —a man who had no inkling of her existence.

She tried to consider her position dispassionately. A romantic practically from birth, Deirdre had always believed in love at first sight and had, in fact, rather hoped that she might one day be privileged to witness it in action. She had been thinking, however, of observing it in Celeste or some other of her sisters, not of having it happen to herself! Now she found that the experience, rather than being sublime and wonderful, as she had always supposed, was in fact rather uncomfortable, even painful.

Deirdre thought over the countless love poems she had committed to memory, trying to draw, from the wisdom of the bards, information she could use for herself. Silently reciting verse after verse, she realized that those who spoke of happiness in love were the same who advocated pursuing it wholeheartedly. She also was reminded of something she already knew from her studies, but now feared she might discover from experience: that unrequited love inspired the most tragic poetry of all.

Dropping her needlework into her lap, Deirdre stared into space, having come to an abrupt decision. She would be a fool to suffer tamely, without ever giving the full glory of love a chance. Clearly, she must make a valiant attempt to storm the citadel of Lord Wrotham's heart. Should that fail, as seemed likely, she would then nobly resign herself to writing the most brilliant and tragic poetry of her life.

She nodded firmly, oblivious to the curious looks she received, and picked up her embroidery only to drop it again. For where would she begin? True, she knew the language of love, chapter and verse, but of the practicalities she knew absolutely nothing. Virtually all of the poetry on the subject dealt with men— gallant knights, for example, battling for the heart of a fair beloved. Of course, that was simply because all of the poets she had memorized were men, she told herself. But the fact remained that she had no idea how to go about capturing a gentleman's heart in the real world of London. She would require assistance. But whose?

The answer to that question was provided a short time later during a nuncheon far superior to the meals served during their first days in residence, proving Marie's selection of a cook to be as sound as her choice of a hairdresser. The butler, a starched-up individual by the name of Smathers, delivered a note to Lady Penrose during the meal. Scanning it quickly, she looked up with a smile.

"Beata is in Town, girls," she announced. "She arrived last night with Mark and little Geoffrey and asks us to come for tea this afternoon. Oh!" Her face suddenly fell. "I nearly forgot that we are already engaged to go to Mrs. Drummond-Burrell's today, Celeste. She most particularly asked last night that I bring you. We dare not risk offending her by crying off, for she is one of the patronesses of Almack's."

"Can we not go see Beata afterwards, Mama, or tomorrow?" asked Celeste. She and Beata had never been particularly close, though she had expressed impatience to see her little nephew.

"Mama," Deirdre broke in suddenly, a plan already forming, "did Mrs. Drummond-Burrell invite me as well?"

Lady Penrose squirmed uncomfortably. "To tell you the truth, Didi, I... I don't believe your name came up. Oh, dear! I suppose you could come along, though it would not be quite the thing." She was obviously torn between protocol and duty to her fourth daughter.

"No, no, Mama, what I was thinking was that I could go to see Beata this afternoon if I needn't go with you."

The Baroness gave a gusty sigh. "Why, certainly you may! You may take the barouche, and don't forget to take Marie along for propriety's sake. I will mention you to Mrs. Drummond-Burrell this afternoon, to be certain that you receive a voucher when Celeste does. I'm sure you will have ever so much gayer a time than we!" She was chattering in her relief, clearly pleased to have the matter so neatly taken care of.

∾

A little before four, Deirdre presented herself on Beata's

doorstep. She was impatient to see her sister again, completely apart from the favour she intended to ask of her. Beata had been the only one of her sisters (except Faith, of course) who seemed to understand her need to write poetry, and who shared the sensitivity to beauty which accompanied that need.

When Beata had married the Honourable Mark Jameson, second son of Earl Dulton, three years ago, she and Deirdre had promised to write regularly —and had, for a while. Deirdre's absent-mindedness and the demands of motherhood on Beata, however, had caused the correspondence to become more sporadic during the past year or so. Therefore, Deirdre had not had news of her sister for some months; she wondered whether she had changed much.

Beata's first words demonstrated that she had not. "Didi, I missed you so! I must admit, when I got Mama's note saying that only you would be coming I was more pleased than disappointed. I expect I'll see more than enough of Mama— and Celeste and Althea, too, for that matter— before the Season is over."

"Bee!" exclaimed Deirdre, choking on a laugh. "I see you are as outspoken as ever. I'm glad, for I admit I am finding the conventions of Town rather, er, constricting." She thought with regret of her daily solitary walks in the country.

"Already?" asked Beata with ready sympathy. "I fear it will get worse. But tell me how everything is with you. How goes the poetry?"

Outwardly, as well, Beata was much the same as Deirdre remembered, her hair a rich honey colour instead of the bright guinea-gold Althea and Celeste possessed. Her figure was still nearly as slender as Deirdre's and she had obviously made good use of her husband's money to enhance her innate sense of style. All in all, Mrs. Jameson was a lovely and extremely elegant woman.

Deirdre told her about sending her collection to Mr. Hunt, startled to realize that she had not even thought about it since last night. "Of course, he has only agreed to look at it, so I daresay I should not get my hopes up."

"I may not be as outspoken in my praise as Faith, but I always thought your poetry quite good," said Beata encouragingly. "I'll not be surprised to see it in print. But never tell me Mama approved of this course?"

"I saw no point in mentioning it to her just yet," replied Deirdre evasively, and was relieved to see Beata nod in agreement.

"Nor will I see fit to mention it," she assured her. Then her deep blue eyes became more piercing, reminding Deirdre that Beata had always seemed to know what she was thinking. "But I don't imagine that's what is bothering you right now, and it is perfectly obvious that something is. Out with it, Didi! Is Celeste becoming puffed up with her success?" She chuckled at Deirdre's expression. "Oh, yes, I've already heard about Althea's 'little' do last night. I haven't let so many connections slip as Mama supposes."

Deirdre shook her head ruefully. "You always did know everything practically before it happened. But no, Celeste is not the problem." Haltingly, she attempted to describe her feelings the night before at the sight of Lord Wrotham. Though she omitted the gentleman's name, she still found great relief in unburdening herself to her most understanding sister. "I know it sounds absurd," she finished. "I mean, I haven't even spoken to the man, and he has no idea that I so much as exist."

But Beata was nodding again. "It was much the same with

Mark and myself. Did I never tell you? I went about engaging his notice quite systematically, once I had selected him from the crowd. I'm not the romantic you are, Didi. I have always felt that Fate does best with a helping hand."

Deirdre laughed again. "You were ever the realist in the family, Bee. And I had thought Mark did the courting!"

"Oh, he did!" Beata hastened to assure her. "He simply needed some encouragement to begin. After that, things went along famously, though he was so shy I believe he nearly drove Mama to distraction. I, however, never doubted how things would turn out." Her eyes twinkled as she smiled smugly. "We'll simply have to do the same for the gentleman you've selected, Didi. But first, you must tell me his name, if you managed to find it out."

Deirdre hesitated, then nodded. "I... I don't know his given name, but he is Lord Wrotham."

Beata sat back abruptly among the satin cushions of the divan and stared at her sister, momentarily speechless. "Wrotham?" she finally gasped. "You've developed a *tendre* for Lord Wrotham?" Then she began to chuckle. "I always did love a challenge, Didi. This Season may be quite interesting, after all."

"Then you'll help me, Bee?" Deirdre's clear grey eyes were pleading.

"Oh, I wouldn't miss it! It's a good thing, you know, that you didn't mention this to Althea. She quite set her cap at him three years back and only accepted poor Bruce when it was perfectly obvious Wrotham wouldn't bite. Obvious to her, that is. I could have told her two months earlier the man wasn't interested, but she's always been a great one for seeing things as she wishes them to be. I hope Mama hasn't turned Celeste's head in his direction yet. She's no more his type than Althea is, as they're practically cut from the same pattern."

"Celeste hasn't seemed particularly interested in him," Deirdre was able to say truthfully, though she knew it was not for want of effort on Lady Penrose's part.

"Good! Now this is what I think we ought to do...."

When Celeste and the baroness arrived an hour later, just as little Geoffrey was brought down from his nap, Beata had a plan to put forth. "Suppose you allow Didi to stay with me for a week or so?" she suggested as her mother bounced her first-born grandson, whom she had never met until that moment, on her knee. Lady Penrose had always adored small children, and did not allow her dignity to interfere with her enjoyment of them.

Startled, Lady Penrose looked from Beata to Deirdre. "With you? Why, whatever for? Though I suppose there would be no harm in it." Actually, the idea appealed so much to her that she wondered why she had not thought of it before. Beata had always seemed to understand Didi so much better than she did herself.

"Of course there would be no harm. I imagine you have your hands amply full with Celeste's come-out, Mama. We wouldn't want Didi neglected." Beata had clearly noticed the contrast between Celeste's attire and Deirdre's.

This admonition struck uncomfortably near home, but Lady Penrose ignored it with a smile. "If Didi would like to stay here, I have no fault to find. You two were ever close, and no doubt will deal famously together. What's that, my little angel?" she cooed, turning her attention back to Geoffrey, considering the matter settled.

When Lady Penrose and her two daughters left a short time later, Beata told Deirdre to be at her house by ten the next morning, bag and baggage. "For we have work to do!" she whispered with a wink.

CHAPTER FIVE

EDISON GATES, FOURTH MARQUIS OF WROTHAM, SET ASIDE the volume of Milton he was perusing with a sigh. "Yes, Bigby? My cousin, I presume?" he asked before his butler could speak.

"Yes, milord," replied Bigby impassively. "Shall I deny you?"

"No, no. I might as well have it out with him sooner rather than later. Show him in." Lord Wrotham rose from his favourite reading chair by the fire and crossed the library to stand behind his desk. It seemed inappropriate for him to be physically at ease during an interview which promised to be most uncomfortable.

A moment later, Bigby reopened the door to admit a portly young man of medium height whose dress proclaimed him an aspirer to the dandy set. His mincing step seemed at odds with his bulk, but when he stopped to put up a quizzing glass to regard the Marquis, the motion was one of controlled grace. Having apparently satisfied himself that the man awaiting him was indeed his cousin, Myron Gates lowered the glass and proceeded to arrange himself elegantly in a chair facing the desk.

"You've come for money again, I make no doubt," stated Wrotham when his cousin remained silently smirking.

"What, no pleasantries?" asked Myron, his voice as affected as his gait. "Can we not at least share a glass of brandy before coming to the mercenary purpose of my visit?"

"You're welcome to a glass," replied the Marquis, nodding at a collection of decanters on the sideboard. "I don't care for it this early in the day, myself." He waited until Myron had availed himself of a generous helping of brandy and repositioned himself in his chair before continuing. "That out of the way, perhaps you can enlighten me as to the reason I should be expected to continue to settle your debts. You have been of age some months now, and might be expected to manage your own affairs. I am no longer responsible for you, morally or financially."

"But Ed," drawled his cousin, leaning as far forward as his girth would allow. "You are the reason I am in debt. It is only fair that you should assist me."

"I?" asked Wrotham in disbelief. What maggot had Myron in his head this time?

"Why, of course. Were I not your heir, the merchants would not be so eager to extend me credit, and I would not be so frequently tempted to oblige them by accepting it," responded Myron in a reasonable tone.

The Marquis snorted. "You do have the one virtue, Myron, of being amusing. Never fear, I shall rectify matters for you."

"Then you'll pay my creditors?" asked Myron complacently. "I knew I could count on you, Ed." He tossed off the rest of his brandy and began to heave himself to his feet to refill the glass when Wrotham's voice stopped him.

"No, Myron, that is not what I meant. Since you claim that being my heir is at the root of your financial irresponsibility, you will be extremely happy to know that I intend to wed before the year is out. That should remove you from temptation's way, I should think."

Myron collapsed back into his chair, his limbs arranged somewhat less elegantly than before. "Marry?" he choked out. "What start is this? Why have I heard nothing?" He made a valiant effort to recover his composure. "And who, pray, is the lucky lady?" he managed to ask with at least a semblance of his usual drawl.

"I have never felt it necessary to keep you apprised of my every action, Myron. You will discover the details along with the rest of the polite world, when they appear in the papers. I am willing to advance you one hundred pounds, which I expect you to repay next quarter, but that is to be the end of my charity. I recommend in the meantime that you endeavour to curtail your spendthrift ways against the day when credit will not be so readily extended." Lord Wrotham handed his cousin a note, then seated himself at his desk and began to go through some papers, indicating that the interview was at an end.

Holding the note in nerveless fingers, Myron silently opened and closed his mouth several times before slowly rising to go. He nearly accused the Marquis of taking this step to spite him, but stopped himself in time. Surely no man, especially one so averse to matrimony as Wrotham was known to be, would marry simply to cut off a kinsman's credit. The idea was absurd. Noticeably lacking the customary mince in his stride, Myron left the library in silence.

Lord Wrotham waited until the door had closed behind his cousin to suspend his activity at the desk.

He heaved a sigh, though not precisely one of relief. For Myron's unspoken suspicion, as it happened, was quite correct: the single reason behind his decision to marry was to replace Myron as his heir. And as yet he had no idea who the "lucky lady" might be.

It was perfectly true that Wrotham had no desire to marry. Until his younger brother's death two years ago in the Napoleonic campaigns, he had never thought it would be necessary. He had intended to remain some years in Italy, where he had made several close friends among the literary circles of that most civilized country, learning more of music, poetry and art. Justin would have made a fine heir.

Myron, however, was another matter entirely. He had shown over the past two years, beginning almost before Justin was cold in his grave, just how quickly he would manage to run through the family fortune were he free to do so. Wrotham had no intention of allowing him that freedom and had there-fore determined to choose a bride from among this Season's crop of young hopefuls. He had returned from the Continent to England, and then to London, for that very purpose, but did not relish the task.

Rising, he crossed from the desk to the sideboard. Perhaps he could use a drop of brandy after all.

∾

"Hmm. The silvery pink, I think," said Beata, critically

surveying the choice of fabrics Madame Sophie's assistant spread before them. "And perhaps another in the powder blue. Yes, that one, with the white spangles." She turned to look back at Deirdre consideringly. "And a few lengths of ribbon to match, please, for her hair." The assistant scurried off to find the required items while Madame Sophie beamed in approval.

"With you and me to guide her, Mrs. Jameson, this one will be most beautiful, and most unusual, *non*? She will do my gowns as much credit as you yourself do, madame."

"More, I hope," replied Beata to the modiste. She had the greatest respect for Madame Sophie's taste, but knew better than to take her flattery to heart. "What think you of this silver reticule to go with the pink?"

Deirdre was finding shopping with Beata a vastly different, and far more satisfying, experience than the same activity with her mother had been. Beata's choices never made her cringe; indeed, she showed an exquisite sense of colour and style that Deirdre could not help but revel in. And her own suggestions, rather than being ignored or ridiculed, were seriously considered and often acted upon. She felt that her growing wardrobe would likely be very becoming indeed.

"Mrs. Jagels will be coming to dress your hair tomorrow after tea," commented Beata as they left the shop. "She claims to have some clever styles to try."

"Mrs. Jagels? Is that not the same hairdresser that Mama has employed?" asked Deirdre in surprise.

"Yes. Marie made a point of telling me yesterday that the woman should have a chance to prove herself on your hair, so I thought we'd give her that chance— without Celeste about to monopolize her," she added so drily that Deirdre wondered what else Marie might have said.

"So," continued Beata briskly, allowing a footman to hand her into the waiting carriage, "your wardrobe is well under way and Mrs. Jagels will doubtless work some of her magic on your hair. Dancing must be the next step, I think."

"Oh, Mama already engaged a dancing master for Celeste and myself. We needn't worry about that," interposed Deirdre hastily. She had not enjoyed those lessons in the least and had no desire for more.

"And I'll wager that Celeste monopolized the dancing master in the same manner she did Mrs. Jagels. How much did you actually learn? Can you waltz, for instance?"

Deirdre hesitated. The dancing master, Mr. Riminoff, was an oily, leering Russian of middle age who repelled her more than a little. In truth, she had not begrudged Celeste the majority of the man's time and had gone to some lengths to avoid waltzing with him. "Not... not very well, I suppose," she answered finally.

"It may surprise you to hear it, but Mark is a superb dancer and will endeavour to instruct you, if that is acceptable. I spoke to him about it last night," Beata informed her with a knowing twinkle.

Deirdre smiled her relief. Mark Jameson was a pleasant man, totally devoted to Beata, and Deirdre felt completely comfortable in his presence. "Thank you," she said. "I will admit I could use some polish in that area."

"I suspected so. Now, have you been taught to use a fan properly?"

∼

Between Beata and Mark, Deirdre was thoroughly instructed

over the next few days in the arts of dancing, flirtation, conversation and even walking, All of the things she had always assumed her other sisters had been born knowing Deirdre was now mastering for herself and found it not nearly so unpleasant as she had feared it would be.

Mrs. Jagels proved herself a wizard indeed. She demonstrated, for Beata's and Deirdre's approval, no fewer than six enchanting styles especially suited to Deirdre's fine, flyaway hair. Deirdre's personal favourite was comprised of intricate braids interwoven with ribbons at the top of her head, with side tendrils pinned so that they fluffed charmingly about her face. And she had always thought only curls could be beautiful!

Beata had decided that the new Deirdre should make her debut on Wednesday at Almack's, to which she had now received a voucher. Lady Penrose and Celeste were to meet them there, and Deirdre would accompany them back to Penrose House afterwards.

"Wrotham will almost certainly not be present, of course," Beata told her during the drive to King Street. "To my knowledge he has never been to Almack's, though of course he has the entree. In fact, he is so rarely in Society, especially in the past year or two, that I have been able to discover less about him than I had hoped to. I believe he has become something of a recluse of late."

Deirdre was more relieved than disappointed at this news. She thought she could do with some practice with her new look and skills in public before encountering him, though she did not say so to Beata for fear that her sister would think her faint-hearted.

When Deirdre mounted the steps to the celebrated

Assembly Rooms on Wednesday night she was conscious that she looked her best, in her new ball gown of silver-pink tissue, her pale hair looped smoothly down and then up into a small knot tied with ribbons and flowers. It was an unusual but delightful sensation to one who had so rarely given any thought to her appearance.

Upon entering, Beata looked at once for her mother and Celeste and spied them on the far side of the large, rather plain ballroom, surrounded by the usual throng of gentlemen vying for Celeste's attention. Smiling in anticipation, she took Deirdre's arm and guided her round the edge of the room so that Lady Penrose would not see them until they were before her. Mr. Jameson, looking even more quietly elegant than usual in the knee-breeches and tails that were *de rigueur* at Almack's, followed.

"Madam," said Beata at the Baroness's elbow, pulling Deirdre from behind her with a flourish and then stepping back, "I should like to present your daughter, Miss Deirdre Wheaton."

Lady Penrose turned with a smile which froze on her face when she beheld Deirdre. Stifling her desire to laugh at her mother's expression, Deirdre sank into a deep curtsy to hide her own smile. Celeste, flirting her fan at some compliment from Sir Malcolm, turned in time to catch the full effect of Deirdre rising from her curtsy— and promptly dropped her fan. As Sir Malcolm vied with two or three other gentlemen for the honour of retrieving it, she found her voice.

"Didi! Just look at you! I vow, Beata, you must be a sorceress to have wrought such a change!" Her delight appeared genuine as she stepped back to better view the transformation which had been worked on her sister.

"Lovely, my dear, perfectly lovely," chimed in Lady Penrose, finding her tongue at last. "You have met Lord Linley, I know, and Sir Malcolm. Let me introduce Mr. Edwards and Mr. Barclay. My daughter Deirdre." As the gentlemen scrambled forward to make the acquaintance of this new beauty, the very tiniest of frowns appeared briefly between Celeste's brows, though her smile never faltered.

The music began at that moment, and Mr. Barclay made haste to claim Deirdre for the first set while Sir Malcolm led Celeste onto the floor. Beata was about to join the dancers with her husband, but Lady Penrose detained her.

"Beata, I must agree with Celeste. However did you work such magic in only a week's time? Deirdre looks nigh as beautiful as her sisters."

"Are you only now noticing that, ma'am?" asked Beata archly before taking Mark's arm to proceed to the floor. Lady Penrose was left to ponder what truth there was to be found in Beata's words. Before she had pondered long, however, she was joined by Althea, who had but that moment arrived, Sir Bruce in tow.

"Good evening, Mama," she greeted the Baroness, lightly kissing her cheek. "I thought you said Didi was to attend tonight. Is she not yet here?" She glanced along the wall, where the dowagers sat with the debutantes who had not been fortunate enough to find partners for the first dance.

"Indeed she is," replied Lady Penrose, gesturing in the direction of the dance floor. She found Althea's expression, once she spotted her young sister, fully as comical as Deirdre had found her own not ten minutes earlier. "Surely you did not expect to see her sitting among the ape-leaders?"

"Good heavens!" Althea managed to say after a moment.

"I dare swear I should have passed her on the street, she is so changed! Mama, we must start our match-making all over again, I fear. Mr. Flinder will never do for her now. Why, he has not even the entree here!" They fell into a comfortable discussion which of Celeste's cast-offs might be the most suitable mate for Deirdre while Sir Bruce wandered off in search of one of the low-stakes card-games available at Almack's.

~

Lord Wrotham glanced about the Assembly Rooms with poorly concealed distaste. He now remembered why he had never returned after his single visit some four years ago, in spite of frequent urging by various of his friends, to include Emily Cowper, one of the patronesses, and the man at his side.

"Come now, Ed, no need to look as though you've swallowed a bug," exclaimed Lord Ellerby, clapping him on the shoulder. "Not so bad as all that. Said you were looking to get leg-shackled, and this is the place for it, right enough."

Wrotham's pained expression intensified. "Need you announce it to the world, Charles? Try for some semblance of decorum, if that's not asking too much." Ellerby was his closest friend, but there was no denying that he could be a bit of a nodcock at unguarded moments.

Charles ran a hand through his already disordered sandy hair. "Sorry, old boy, you're perfectly right. Won't do to have word get about you're hanging out for a wife. The old tabbies would never give you a minute's peace."

"Precisely." Wrotham was gratified that Charles understood so readily. Of course, Ellerby himself had been on the receiving end of the machinations of his share of match-making mamas, so he spoke from experience.

That experience, in fact, was why Wrotham had chosen to share his plan with the Earl, apart from their close friendship. Never having seriously considered courting a woman of his own class before, he realized that he hadn't the least idea how to go about it and would need an advisor. He glanced sidelong at Charles, hoping that he had chosen wisely.

"Now," said Wrotham in an undertone intended to inspire Ellerby to be equally soft-spoken, "what can you tell me about this Season's crop of Incomparables?"

Charles took the hint, whispering his reply. "Not all Incomparables, of course, Ed, but I can see that you might want to limit your choice to the best lookers. Let me see." He surveyed the room critically, though without the use of a quizzing glass, an affectation both he and Wrotham despised. "There's Miss Millington, Glenstoke's daughter, making her come-out this Season. A real little beauty, if a bit on the plump side. Then there's Mary Jeffcoat, here for her second try. Can't think why she didn't take last year, unless it's that she hasn't a brain in her head. Still, who looks for wit in a wife? Then there's—"

"I may as well tell you at once, Charles," interrupted the Marquis, "that beauty is only one, and by no means the chief, attribute I shall look for in a wife. I, for one, could not bear to be bound for life to some lovely peagoose."

Charles nodded, though his expression was quizzical. "Looking for a bluestocking, then, Ed? I'd forgotten you were such a scholar. Let me see..."

"No, no, I didn't say that! It's simply... oh, never mind. Who else is here?"

"Well, I heard Lady Thumble is bringing out a younger

sister this year. Haven't seen the chit yet, as I wasn't in Town in time for her card-party last week, but if she bears a family resemblance she should be quite tolerable. Ah! There is Althea now!" Before Wrotham could stop him, Ellerby waved at Lady Thumble, who stood nearby with her mother, and advanced towards her. The Marquis had no choice but to follow.

Lord Wrotham remembered all too vividly Lady Thumble's pursuit of him when she had made her debut three years earlier. She had been beautiful, of course, but her empty chatter had soon palled. Her sister, now a Mrs. Jameson, he recalled, had evinced more intelligence, but had shown no interest in himself, and he had not taken the trouble to scrape an acquaintance with her, especially since it would have meant spending more time in Althea's presence.

He had regretted his decision to attend Lady Thumble's card-party last week almost as soon as he arrived, and had received the distinct impression that this Season's Miss Wheaton was to be thrown at him by Lady Penrose as vigorously as her eldest daughter had been before. Both in looks and character, he had found Miss Celeste Wheaton depressingly similar to her sister.

"So happy to see you again, Lord Wrotham," Lady Thumble was saying, echoed by her mother. "You have met my sister Celeste, who I believe is engaged on the dance floor. But let me present you to Didi— rather, I should say, to Miss Deirdre Wheaton, my next youngest sister, who is also in London for the Season." She beckoned to the aforementioned sister, who was at that moment returning on Mr. Barclay's arm from the minuet just concluded.

Miss Deirdre Wheaton was certainly attractive, Wrotham observed as she approached. Nor did she particularly resemble Lady Thumble, being both fairer and built on less generous lines. Though her colour increased slightly as Lady Thumble introduced her, he was pleased to note that Miss Wheaton did not simper as she dropped a perfect curtsey to him.

"I am pleased to make your acquaintance, my lord." Her voice was as light and pleasing as her form.

"Charmed, Miss Wheaton," murmured Wrotham to the vision in rose and silver before him. "Would you care to dance?"

CHAPTER SIX

WHEN DEIRDRE HAD SEEN THE MARQUIS STANDING BY HER sister, regarding her with those remarkably piercing dark eyes, her heart had immediately begun to pound, but she remembered Beata's training in time and strove to allow no trace of her disquiet to show in her expression. Even when he asked her to dance, she managed to accept calmly and coolly, despite her riotous thoughts.

But when the strains of a waltz began, she wondered frantically whether her careful control could withstand that test. Such was the combined influence of Lady Thumble, Mrs. Jameson and Lady Penrose that Deirdre had the permission of the patronesses to dance it, but she trembled none the less. This would be her first public waltz, circumstance enough for nervousness without taking her partner into consideration. Would he notice her inexperience?

"Pray forgive me if I tread on your feet, Miss Wheaton," said the Marquis as he swept her into the dance. "It has been some time since I last danced."

Deirdre was startled into a genuine smile at his remark, so in tune with her own feelings.

Wrotham was dazzled by the sweetness of that smile. Was it his imagination, or was this girl something special? Not that he could possibly know that after less than five minutes in her company, he chided himself quickly. It was certainly no part of his plan to fall head over ears for the first schoolroom miss he danced with.

"Is this your first visit to London?" he asked after a moment, hoping to see that smile again and perhaps to learn something about this enchanting creature beyond her family connections.

"Yes, it is," replied Miss Wheaton, her low-pitched voice charming him again. "Have you spent many Seasons here, my lord?"

They spoke on such impersonal topics until the dance ended. By the time Lord Wrotham returned her to Lady Penrose, he was most favourably impressed, though he still knew little about Miss Wheaton beyond her looks and pleasant voice. To his surprise, he heard himself asking permission to call upon her the next day.

"Why, certainly you may, my lord!" exclaimed Lady Penrose before her daughter could answer. "We shall look forward to your visit."

Wrotham bowed and turned away, reflecting that the mother would be a definite thorn to deal with, were he to pursue this particular rose. He snorted to himself at his use of such a poetic metaphor. Having an intense respect and admiration for the great poets, he had an equally intense dislike for upstarts who pretended to compose verse. He was not about to become one of them at the sight of a pretty face.

"You look thoughtful, Ed," commented Ellerby, returning from the floor at that moment, whither he had partnered Lady Thumble for the waltz. "Does that bode ill or fair?"

The Marquis forced a disinterested smile. "For whom?" he asked rhetorically. Before his friend could answer, he changed the subject. "Did you find Lady Thumble all that you remembered?"

"And more," replied Charles with a sigh. "She's the one woman who might have persuaded me out of bachelorhood, I believe. But when she was out three years ago I hadn't yet succeeded to m'title, and didn't have the presumption to pursue her as mere Mr. Trent. Timing is everything, Ed, every-thing." He spoke with unwonted seriousness, making Wrotham regard his usually happy-go-lucky friend with some concern.

"Not trying to brew something behind old Thumble's back, are you, Charles?" he asked cautiously. That could prove awkward for his own case.

"Behind— good lord, no, Ed! How can you say so? She's as cheerful and friendly as ever, I'll grant you, but gave no hint she'd be interested in so much as a flirtation. How prospers your search?" Charles seemed anxious to drop what was apparently a painful subject.

"Slowly," replied Wrotham with a smile, hoping to lighten his friend's mood. "If I'm to have a field to choose from, you'll need to introduce me about a bit quicker."

Lord Ellerby proceeded to introduce him to more young hopefuls than Wrotham could possibly remember, though he made a point to dance with one or two who seemed less affected or more attractive than the others. As face after lovely face passed before him, however, his mind's eye kept returning to that of his first acquaintance of the evening.

To divert his thoughts from Miss Wheaton, he began to consider what Ellerby had said earlier. If it were true that Lady Thumble was the type of woman he desired, Charles must definitely meet the other Wheaton girl— what was her name? Celine? Something like that.

Unfortunately, that young lady was already engaged for every dance, and so constantly surrounded by gentlemen that rudeness would have been necessary to get near her. In addition, Ellerby seemed to be deliberately keeping a discreet distance from Lady Thumble since their earlier conversation.

No doubt there would be other opportunities, however. It was only the start of the Season, after all.

Sir Malcolm, at least, was not making a fool of himself over Deirdre, Celeste was pleased to note as he led her out for the second time that evening. Not only was he the handsomest of her suitors, he flattered and flirted most outrageously, especially when Lady Penrose was not in evidence, which she found strangely exciting. He was ever so much more interesting than prosy Lord Linley, she thought.

Celeste was genuinely happy at her sister's sudden success, even if the defection of some half dozen of her admirers was somewhat disappointing. She rightly credited it to their fickleness, however, and not to any intent on Deirdre's part; she knew her sister too well to believe her capable of any sort of underhandedness.

"A penny for your thoughts, sweet lady," murmured Sir Malcolm, recapturing her attention.

"I was just thinking about Didi," replied Celeste artlessly. "The change in her is so striking!"

"She cannot hold a candle to you, my sweet," Sir Malcolm assured her, holding her more closely than was strictly necessary, even for the waltz. "You possess ten times her charm for me." He rubbed his thumb along the back of her hand, sending a tingle up her spine.

Lady Penrose, watching from the edge of the floor, frowned. She would have to speak to Celeste about so encouraging one of the least eligible of her admirers.

Deirdre, meanwhile, was enjoying the evening much more than she had expected to. Once the nervousness of that first waltz with Lord Wrotham was out of the way, she was able to relax and take pleasure in the rest of the evening. It was a heady experience to find herself nearly as sought-after as Celeste, and she would not have been female had she not enjoyed it. True, none of the other gentlemen who danced and flirted with her affected her pulse in the same way as Lord Wrotham, but they were all very pleasant, none the less.

"It is as I told you, Didi," commented Beata at one point when they were both enjoying much-needed glasses of lemonade. "You are not the ugly duckling at all. You were simply a cygnet waiting for the right moment to become a swan."

"Along with a bit of help from a certain dear sister," added Deirdre with a fond smile for Beata. "I confess, I never really believed you until tonight."

"Will you be trading in your pens and verses for the whirl of Society now that you have seen what it is like?" asked Beata with interest.

Deirdre blinked in surprise. She had not thought of her poetry at all during the past few hours. "Can I not do both, become something even more out of the ordinary?" she asked only half-teasingly. Give up her poetry? Never!

"The Rhyming Reigning Belle, eh?" asked Beata. "That *would* be original."

"I like to think that what I write goes a bit beyond simple rhyming," returned Deirdre with a frown, not quite ready to have her poetry made so light of. "Perhaps I will keep it to myself for the present, after all."

That conversation lingered in Deirdre's mind for the remainder of the evening, however. Suppose the Marquis of Wrotham was not even literary, or wrote dreadful stuff, such as what Mr. Flinder had given her to read? Suppose he had never even heard of Milton or Spenser? Would she still wish to capture his heart?

Looking towards the door, where Lord Wrotham was taking his leave at that moment, she saw him turn in her direction, and their glances met for a brief instant. Deirdre's pulse began to race again, all but driving those pressing questions from her head. She would simply have to find out what his likes and dislikes were, and the extent of his education, at the next opportunity, she decided. There would be time enough then to call off her plan— wouldn't there?

Back at Penrose House the next morning, the bouquets delivered were not exclusively for Celeste, though her admirers still predominated. Deirdre received offerings from Mr. Barclay and Lord Linley, among others, though those diplomatic gentlemen did not forget Celeste in the throes of their new admiration for her sister.

Lady Penrose was sincerely delighted with the miracle Beata had wrought with their ugly duckling, though she was careful not to phrase her pleasure so. To think that Lord Wrotham had actually asked to call upon her! In truth, she could not understand why he should be so taken with Didi while barely glancing at Celeste, but she would be the last one to question the workings of Fate, especially when it worked in her favour. If he could be brought to make an offer for Didi, it would be far, far more than she had ever dared to hope for.

"Mama, may we ride, or perhaps walk, in the Park this afternoon?" asked Deirdre over breakfast. "We are 'out' now, are we not?" She was trying to focus on anything other than Lord Wrotham's impending visit, which had her in a quake, though she was not certain why. Besides, she really did want to go walking. Used to outdoor freedom all her life, she found that being penned indoors for two entire weeks was beginning to wear on her nerves. No doubt that was the true cause of her fidgets, she decided.

"I don't see why not, Didi," answered Lady Penrose. "I can arrange for a pair of ladies' riding horses to be sent round on approval for you and Celeste tomorrow, and today, if the weather remains fine, we can drive out in the open barouche."

"Oh, Mama, Sir Malcolm is taking me driving today. Had you forgotten?" interposed Celeste, drawing a frown from her mother.

"I shall thank you not to agree to any more outings without my approval, Celeste," said the Baroness severely. "Nor is it wise to give Sir Malcolm such encouragement."

"Why, what is wrong with Sir Malcolm?" asked Celeste in surprise. "You never objected to his calling here."

"Nothing is precisely *wrong* with him. It is simply that you can do better. It is common knowledge that Sir Malcolm's pockets are frequently to let, besides which he has quite a reputation as a flirt. You would not wish people to think you *fast*."

"Of... of course not, Mama," replied Celeste, appearing somewhat deflated. "Though I must say I have not *seen* him flirting with ... with anyone else. May I still go driving with him this afternoon?"

"Since you have already engaged to do so, I suppose you must. But do try to give equal attention to some of your more eligible suitors, Celeste. Remember, your dowry is not over-large." Lady Penrose forebore saying more on the subject; more than one young lady had been known to develop a tendre for a man simply because her parents did not care for him.

Deirdre was only half attending to their conversation. Instead, she was mentally rehearsing the questions she meant to work into her conversation with Lord Wrotham that morning. She hoped she would be able to remember them when faced with his actual presence.

∿

"What drivel!" exclaimed Wrotham, throwing down the latest copy of the *Examiner*. Lord Ellerby, who was breakfasting with him that morning, looked up questioningly.

"Something wrong, Ed?" he asked mildly.

Wrotham snorted. "If Hunt is going to undertake to print

poetry, the least he can do is cull out the chaff! I will admit he occasionally finds a gem from an unknown, but more often than not, it seems, what he passes off as poetry is no more than the moonings of a lovesick schoolboy. He must have owed this Mr. Glennis a favour."

"Glennis?" echoed Charles absently, finishing the last of his kidneys. "Some connection of his wife's, I believe."

"That explains it then." Even when he was not attending, and Wrotham knew that poetry never held Ellerby's interest, Charles was able to reel off the exact relationship of everyone in London to everyone else. In that capacity, if in no other, his memory for detail was astonishing, Wrotham had to admit. It was such unexpected flashes of intelligence which endeared him to the more scholarly Marquis. He himself often had trouble remembering the name of whatever person he was speaking to.

"Shall we be off?" Wrotham asked, standing.

"Whatever you say, Ed. Still can't see why I have to tag along, though. I ain't the one looking to hang up the ladle."

"I need you to give me courage, Charles," replied Wrotham lightly, earning a snort of disbelief from his friend. He had decided against telling Ellerby about the resemblance of the elder Miss Wheaton to Lady Thumble for fear he would set his hopes too high. He was bringing him along to meet the girl, but that was as far as his match-making attempts would go.

~

When Lord Wrotham and Lord Ellerby entered the main drawing-room of Penrose House, it was to discover some half-dozen callers ahead of them. Glancing over to where Deirdre sat conversing with Mr. Barclay and Lord Naseby, he found that she looked even lovelier, if possible, than she had looked last night, with her hair piled loosely on top of her head and gowned in cerulean blue. Before availing himself of a seat near her, however, he and Charles paid their respects to their hostess.

"Lady Penrose, I trust you will forgive my descending upon you without warning," said Lord Ellerby with a charming smile. "I am a great admirer of Lady Thumble and wished to meet her lovely mother and sisters."

The Baroness, not yet old enough to be immune to flattery, dimpled at his words. "I remember you of course, my lord. I recollect you were a Mr. Trent when last I was in London."

"Yes, my uncle, the third Earl, was still living then," replied Ellerby. "I am gratified that you should recall so much about me."

Judging by her speculative expression, Lady Penrose had quickly searched her memory and concluded that if Lord Ellerby had inherited his uncle's fortune as well as his title, he must be very well to grass. "Let me introduce you to my daughter Celeste," she said smoothly.

That accomplished, Lord Wrotham felt free to turn his attention to the younger Miss Wheaton. While inexperienced in courtship, he was unafflicted with any diffidence regarding his own sex and was able, with a single, pointed glance at his pocket-watch, to remind Mr. Barclay that his quarter hour had expired. Wrotham availed himself of the chair thus vacated, seating himself with a smile next to Miss Deirdre.

"Good morning, Miss Wheaton," he said cordially. "You are looking well today," he added, feeling that a compliment of some sort was probably called for.

"Oh, I am rarely ill, my lord," she responded guilelessly, then suddenly seemed to realize what he had meant to say. "Ah, thank you, my lord," she finished, with a twinkle in her clear grey eyes which caused Lord Wrotham to chuckle as it struck him how his "compliment" had sounded. Deirdre joined in his laughter and the ice between them was effectively broken.

"What I suppose I should have said, Miss Wheaton, is that that colour suits you," said Wrotham after a moment.

"Thank you, my lord, but do not trouble yourself to search for pretty phrases. I am not one to fish after compliments, I assure you," replied Deirdre sincerely. She had noticed, and rather deplored, that tendency in Celeste and had no wish for Lord Wrotham to think her equally vain.

"That is a relief, I must admit," returned the Marquis with a smile. "I often find myself at a loss when a well-turned phrase is called for."

"Oh?" Deirdre realized suddenly that he was giving her the opening she had both hoped for and feared. "And what think you of the well-turned phrases of others?" She couldn't quite bring herself to say "poetry"—it would be too much like an admission, she thought.

To her dismay, Lord Wrotham frowned at her words. "Frequently, I find, the owner of the phrase thinks it far better than it is," he said decidedly. "Why, some of the drivel I've seen in the *Examiner* that is pleased to call itself poetry... well, it should never have been uttered aloud, much less set to paper for the whole world to see."

Deirdre must have looked as stricken as she felt, for he stopped and said, "I apologize, Miss Wheaton. You have touched on something that is a particular aversion of mine, and I fear I over-reacted. What think you of the chances for rain?"

Deirdre hardly knew how she answered him. His nearness to her made it difficult to concentrate, but one thought spun repeatedly through her brain: Lord Wrotham had an aversion to poetry! He had actually said so. Hard on the heels of that unpleasant discovery came another: she still found herself as disturbingly affected by him as ever.

After a few minutes more of conversation on general topics, to which Deirdre contributed very little, the Marquis took his leave of her. He beckoned to Lord Ellerby, who seemed reluctant to rise from his chair by Celeste's side, and the two gentlemen departed.

Mr. Flinder was announced just as they were leaving, and his first words to Deirdre made her very glad that he had not arrived a moment sooner.

"Have you had a chance to look over those verses I left with you, Didi?" he asked, taking the chair Lord Wrotham had so recently (and mercifully!) vacated. "You must tell me what you thought. And when am I to have the honour of seeing a sample of your poetry?"

CHAPTER SEVEN

"MY POETRY?" ASKED DEIRDRE DISTRACTEDLY, BUT MR. Flinder was not attending. His eyes were fixed on her face in something akin to wonder.

"D-Didi? Er, Miss Wheaton? What have, I mean, you... you look quite lovely!" He actually stood again so as to better survey the change in her appearance.

Deirdre felt herself blushing at his frank regard. "Pray, sit down, Mr. Flinder. I have simply had my hair styled differently and put on a new gown, so you needn't goggle so. I am still the same person."

Mr. Flinder sat back down quickly, murmuring an apology, but still his eyes were riveted to her face as if he could not believe what they told him. After another moment of rapt regard, he suddenly grasped her hand and brought it to his lips. Deirdre snatched it away at once with a frown, wondering what could have possessed him so.

"I cannot help myself, Didi," he told her softly. "You are simply divine."

Deirdre felt her temper rising. Jonas had not seemed to regard her in a loverlike manner before, but simply as a friend. It irked her that a mere change in her appearance should so affect his attitude towards her. "That is enough, Jonas," she said sharply. "I believe you wanted my opinion of your work?"

"Yes, yes of course," he said as if coming out of a dream. "And now I will undoubtedly be inspired to write even more. Your beauty is poetry itself."

"Please do not on my account. I rather think you should first turn your attention to improving that which you have already written." She rushed into a franker critique than she had intended to give him, to forestall any more such compliments. She listed the defects she had discovered in his imagery, conflicting moods, even his basic rhyme and metre.

"You didn't like it," he stated flatly, his eyes on the floor, when she had finished. At the sudden constraint in his manner, she belatedly realized that she had mortally offended him.

"I didn't precisely say that," protested Deirdre, inadvertently doing more harm than good. She bit her lip in frustration. "You told me you wanted my honest opinion," she reminded him.

"Very well," said Jonas curtly, "now you must let me critique some of your work. Fair is fair. Though I doubt someone like you— " his eyes raked over her again, this time scathingly "—could do as well as a man." His eyes narrowed. "Do you really write poetry at all? Or was that merely a fable to ensnare me?"

Stung, Deirdre stood abruptly. "One moment, please," she said haughtily and flounced out of the room, drawing interested stares from the other occupants of the drawing-room. In a minute or two, she was back, a sheaf of paper in her hand.

"Here, sir, are your own verses, along with two of my own. You may tell me your opinion— your honest opinion— at Lady Millbanke's tomorrow night. And now I bid you good day."

Jonas frowned uncertainly, suddenly understanding that he had alienated, perhaps beyond repair, this girl who stood to be so useful to him. He had counted on his poetry to impress her; obviously, it had not, and now his anger, born of wounded vanity, had betrayed him. Since she had patently dismissed him, Jonas stood slowly, but made an effort to retrieve matters.

"Didi, I—" he began, but she cut him off.

"I believe I would prefer to be 'Miss Wheaton' after all, Mr. Flinder. Good day," she repeated.

"I'll see you at Lady Millbanke's, Miss Wheaton," he said with a sketchy bow and departed, along with the last of Celeste's morning callers.

"Now whatever was that about, Didi?" asked Celeste avidly when only the Penrose ladies remained in the drawing-room. "Was Mr. Flinder jealous of Lord Wrotham?"

"Lord Wrotham?" echoed Deirdre. Her anger at Mr. Flinder had driven thoughts of the Marquis and the dilemma he presented from her head momentarily, but now they flooded back. "No, of course not," she said vaguely, her mind busy. "If you will excuse me, I have some embroidery to do in my chamber." Leaving her mother and sister to blink in confusion after her, Deirdre slowly walked out of the room.

Alone in her bedchamber, Deirdre actually did fish a piece

of embroidery out of the work bag next to the comfortable chair she sank into. She had always composed more readily while her hands were thus occupied, and hoped that the stitchery would similarly assist clarity of thought now. For surely she needed it more than ever before.

She thought about her resentment earlier that Mr. Flinder should act so differently because of the way she looked; but wasn't the same true of Lord Wrotham? Her grand plan to attract him seemed to have worked. She had his interest, if not yet his love, but did she really want it? Always, she had thought those who made judgements based on appearances must be shallow people, not worth knowing —but what did Lord Wrotham know of her beyond her face and clothes?

And what did she know of him beyond his handsome, athletic exterior, except that he despised poetry? For as long as she could remember, Deirdre's life had revolved around her poetry. It was—or had been— everything to her. And now, its pre-eminence in her life was in danger of being usurped by Lord Wrotham, a man she barely knew, and yet was irresistibly drawn to. What was she to do?

The obvious solution, she told herself, was to have nothing more to do with the Marquis. She could pretend he had never existed, had never played havoc with her emotions. It was absurd to think she might give up her beloved poetry for some fashionable gentleman who undoubtedly preferred cock-fights and horse-racing to a good book.

But then the compelling face of that particular fashionable gentleman swam before the tambour she was busily embroidering and her resolution wavered. After all, within her own family she had done most of her composing in secret. Why could she not continue to do so? Involuntarily, her anguish gave rise to a rhyme in her head.

Deirdre had read that writing poetry had been a kind of release for more than one of the great poets, making suffering, especially the suffering of unrequited love, more bearable; perhaps it would do the same for her. Putting aside her embroidery, she moved to the desk and allowed her thoughts and feelings to flow through her pen.

"I wouldn't have believed it possible, but she's even more beautiful than Lady Thumble was three years ago," Ellerby was saying for at least the third time since he and Wrotham had left Penrose House. "And every bit as engaging. There's a certain innocence, a *joie de vivre* that I never noticed in Althea, as well. She spoke to me as much as to anyone else there, I think, though she'd only just met me. Do you think she likes me, Ed?"

"Assuredly, Charles. How could she help it, such a charming fellow as you are? Your only fault is a tendency to rattle on a bit." He hoped his friend would take the hint and leave him to his thoughts for a few minutes, but he was doomed to disappointment.

"I can't think why I never thought to ask Lady Thumble if she had a sister. I mean, besides Mrs. Jameson, of course, since she is already married."

Wrotham lengthened his stride. As the day was fine, they had chosen to walk the few blocks separating his imposing residence in Berkeley Square from Penrose House on Mount

Street. "So you intend to make Miss Wheaton an offer, do you Charles?" he asked with a sidelong glance at his friend.

As he had expected, the question brought Ellerby up short. "An offer? I say, Ed, hadn't thought that far ahead. Not hanging out for a wife, after all. Still a young man and all that." They continued on in the silence Lord Wrotham had craved, both gentlemen now deep in thought.

In spite of, or perhaps because of, its apparent success, Wrotham was already regretting his first attempt at match-making. He feared that he might have done his friend a disservice by subjecting him to the charms of Celeste Wheaton, who was so like the idealized lost love Ellerby had been lamenting for three years. If he were to marry the girl, would she be constantly compared to her elder sister? That hardly seemed fair.

And then there was Charles. He appeared to be thoroughly besotted by a girl he knew nothing of apart from her beautiful face and pleasant drawing-room manners. That was hardly a basis for a lasting alliance.

Wrotham nearly stopped in his tracks as the realization hit him. Was that not precisely what was happening to himself? What did he know of Miss Deirdre Wheaton that Charles did not know of Celeste? Nothing, he was forced to answer. There was an intelligence in her eyes, her expression, that made him wish to know her better, but he could not be sure after less than half an hour's conversation whether it truly existed or not. She could be as stupid as a cow for all he had been able to discover so far.

But she was certainly prettier than one, he could not help thinking with a smile. Remembering her face, the way she turned her head, he felt a warm glow coursing through him.

Was this love? He had heard the poets describe it so, but had never quite believed in it for mere mortals like himself. A gentleman married for breeding or wealth, preferably choosing a partner that would not irritate him unduly over the course of a lifetime together. That was certainly what he had intended to do. Love had never been a part of his plan.

Looking up, he realized that they were drawing near to his house and pushed away such thoughts. As he had said to himself last night, the Season was only beginning. There would be ample time to decide what he should do about Miss Deirdre Wheaton.

Why then, did he feel so impatient?

After venting her feelings on paper, Deirdre felt somewhat calmer. Without so much as looking over what she had written, she folded the pages in two and tucked them between some blank sheets of paper in the desk drawer.

During the noon meal, Lady Penrose and Celeste were deep in plans for the double ball (as Celeste had dubbed it) which was to be held in two weeks' time. To Deirdre's relief, they seemed to have forgotten her odd behaviour of that morning, for on reflection she realized how distracted she must have appeared. She had no desire to be asked questions to which she had not yet formulated answers.

"How soon shall we send out invitations, Mama?" Celeste was asking.

"As soon as we have our guest list assembled, I should think," replied Lady Penrose. "That way, instead of working our ball around the other events of the Season, everyone else will be forced to work around us."

"But suppose the Prince or some duchess has planned a ball for that same night?" asked Celeste apprehensively. "Would not everyone then shun ours? I should be mortified if my... our come-out ball is not a crush."

"If necessary, we can change the date, even after the invitations are sent out," conceded the Baroness. "It has been done before. But you are already such a success, my dear, that I dare swear many people would rather be here than at one of Prinny's dull dos. It is not unheard of, by any means, to attend two or even three parties in an evening. We shall be forced to do so ourselves before the Season is out, I assure you."

This reassurance seemed to allay Celeste's fears and she fell to discussing the guest list. "Lord Ellerby, that friend of Lord Wrotham's who called this morning, was very nice, I think, Mama. May we invite him? Of course, he is not so handsome as Sir Malcolm, but—" She broke off, clearly remembering what her mother had said that morning and preferring not to provoke more strictures about Sir Malcolm.

"Surely we may," replied Lady Penrose, ignoring Celeste's last remark. "He is very highly placed in the ton and quite eligible. And a friend of Lord Wrotham's, as well." This with a significant glance in Deirdre's direction, which that young lady carefully pretended not to notice.

Deirdre had no wish to elevate her mother's hopes until she had made up own mind about the man. She bent her thoughts to doing just that as Celeste continued to chatter about the ball throughout the remainder of the meal.

~

That afternoon, shortly before five, Sir Malcolm called to take Celeste driving, as arranged. He was shown into the drawing-room, where Lady Penrose sat with her two daughters, Celeste resplendent in a canary-yellow carriage dress with vivid green-and-orange trim and Deirdre, busily embroidering, gowned in a shade of lavender which set off her pale colouring to perfection.

"Good day, Sir Malcolm," said the Baroness, inclining her head as he executed a leg to her. "Do sit with us for a moment before you go. Peters, a word with you." She beckoned to the footman who had shown their visitor in.

As Sir Malcolm seated himself amiably next to Celeste to pick up the thread of the conversation they had been enjoying last night at Almack's, Lady Penrose said something in an undertone to the footman, who nodded and quickly left the room. He reappeared a moment later with the answer to her ladyship's question, and she narrowed her eyes slightly and dismissed him with a motion of her head.

"Sir Malcolm," she said, breaking into his *tete-a-tete* with Celeste, "would you mind terribly taking Didi along as well? She has expressed a desire to see the Park and I had promised to take her this afternoon, but I find myself rather too tired just now."

Deirdre and Celeste both regarded their mother with surprise, as Lady Penrose was not in the habit of admitting to fatigue, but Sir Malcolm seemed to see nothing strange in the request. His smile was a shade less broad, however, as he answered, "Of course, my lady, it would be an honour."

Lady Penrose smiled and thanked him, quite satisfied. That would teach him to attempt to take her Celeste driving without his groom along to bear them company! Obviously, she had been right in her assessment of the man all along.

Still regarding her mother curiously, Deirdre rose. "I'll just run upstairs for my pelisse, then, and shall join you in a moment." She clearly had no idea what Lady Penrose was about, but knew better than to question her in front of a guest.

Celeste might have her suspicions of her mother's motives, but remained silent on the point, instead turning her attention to charming Sir Malcolm out of any ill humour the Baroness's request might have engendered.

Sir Malcolm, however, seemed not to be particularly perturbed at the arrangement when he found himself situated between the two sisters on the seat of his phaeton. Taking up the ribbons, he put the matched bays into a brisk trot and made for the Park.

Deirdre looked about her with interest, trying to ignore the fact that she was undoubtedly an unwanted third in the party. She had been watching Sir Malcolm carefully, bearing in mind what her mother had said that morning, and was beginning to believe that Celeste could indeed do better. Not that wealth was so very important, of course, but Sir Malcolm's smooth way with a compliment implied that he had practiced them on a great many ladies, and Celeste deserved a husband devoted only to her.

Deirdre found the Park delightful, with its trees, small ponds and stretches of grassland criss-crossed by bridle-roads, carriage-ways and footpaths. She resolved to return, soon and frequently, to walk here— though preferably at a less crowded hour. Most of the fashionable world seemed now assembled, riding, walking and rolling slowly by, stopping frequently to nod, speak or gossip with one another. Both sisters were recognized by numerous acquaintances and Deirdre marvelled at this evidence that they already knew so many people in London.

Having exchanged greetings with Lady Heatherton and Julia, who were taking the air in an open barouche, Deirdre turned to make a comment to Celeste when she saw riding towards them the Marquis of Wrotham, astride an enormous grey. He was accompanied by a portly young man she had not previously met, riding a smaller chestnut that seemed barely up to his weight. She was just trying to decide whether to speak first or to wait for him to acknowledge them when he spied her and rode forward with a delighted smile.

"Miss Wheaton!" Lord Wrotham exclaimed. "I did not know you planned to drive in the Park today."

"Good day, Lord Wrotham," replied Deirdre, striving not to blush at the frank admiration in his gaze. "Have you met Sir Malcolm Digby?" She was startled at the abrupt change in his expression.

"Indeed. Digby," replied Lord Wrotham with a curt nod, his displeasure evident.

"Good day, Wrotham," returned Sir Malcolm, his expression all that was civil and proper. "And Mr. Gates. I have not seen you about this week past, Myron."

"Been a tad short of funds," drawled Wrotham's pudgy companion peevishly. "Perhaps you could prevail—"

"Well, we mustn't keep you," broke in Wrotham almost rudely. He seemed upset about something, but Deirdre could not imagine what. "You'll be at Lady Millbanke's tomorrow, Miss Wheaton?" She nodded. "I'll... I'll hope to see you there, then." He appeared to want to add something, but after an infinitesimal pause, he set his mouth in a hard line and rode on.

Myron Gates raised his quizzing glass to scrutinize the occupants of Sir Malcolm's phaeton, his gaze lingering thoughtfully on Deirdre, before following Lord Wrotham more slowly.

CHAPTER EIGHT

LADY MILLBANKE'S WAS THE FIRST IMPORTANT BALL OF THE
Season and, as such, drew everyone who was anyone to see
and be seen by their contemporaries. The Millbanke house, an
imposing residence in Grosvenor Square, was reputed to boast
the largest ballroom in London and Lord Millbanke, an influ-
ential man in government circles, was no more inclined to let it
go to waste than was his sociable wife.

As at Almack's two nights ago, Celeste was immediately
surrounded by her retinue of admirers. She was wearing one
of her few white gowns, though it was not precisely demure,
trimmed as it was with scarlet and royal blue. Deirdre had
refrained from commenting on her sister's patriotism; after all,
both France and the new United States of America shared
those colours.

Also as before, several of Celeste's erstwhile followers
gravitated into Deirdre's somewhat smaller orbit, notably Mr.
Barclay and Lord Linley, as well as Mr. Flinder, who had
rushed to her side the moment their party was announced. He

hastened to inform her that she was looking particularly fetching, in her new gown of palest ice blue.

"If you are not yet engaged for the first dance, would you be so kind as to honour me?" he asked eagerly. "I do so want to get back into your good graces!"

The soulful look on his face was almost comical and, as no one else had yet had opportunity to put his name on her dance card, Deirdre assented with a smile. She had never been able to carry a grudge, and had already forgiven Jonas his ill temper of the day before; after all, she had been rather harsh about his poetry, and she doubted that she would enjoy such criticism any more than he had.

Mr. Barclay then petitioned to sign her card, as did Lord Linley and two or three other gentlemen present in the circle about Deirdre and her sister. Her dance card began to fill, and she had not yet so much as seen Lord Wrotham, she realized in sudden panic. What if he did not come until all of her dances were taken? Or, worse, what if he did not come at all? He had not actually asked her to save him a dance, but still...

At that moment, Lord Wrotham was announced. He took a flatteringly direct route to Deirdre's side and bowed elegantly over her hand. "That colour suits you," he said, which somehow satisfied her more than the flowery compliments the other gentlemen had been lavishing upon her. "Dare I hope your first dance is still free?"

"Sorry, Wrotham, I was ahead of you there," broke in Mr. Flinder triumphantly before Deirdre could answer. "Latecomers don't stand a chance with a diamond like Miss Wheaton."

Deirdre shot Jonas an annoyed glance before holding out her card to the Marquis. "I do have a few dances still unclaimed, my lord," she murmured, careful not to appear too eager. Beata had warned her on that score; and besides, she still had some thinking to do about Lord Wrotham. She hoped that her mind might be more settled by the end of the evening.

"Ah, the second waltz, if I may, and might I ask for the supper dance as well?" asked Wrotham, scribbling his name in both spaces before she could refuse, had she been so inclined.

Instead, she smiled her assent, and he bowed and turned away quickly to do some thinking of his own.

What had possessed him to claim two dances? he wondered. There were undoubtedly many here that would see it as showing a most particular interest, Lady Penrose included. Glancing across to where Charles was hovering over Celeste, he hoped that his friend would limit himself to two dances, or he'd find the announcement in the papers before he knew it. Catching his eye, he beckoned to Ellerby, who came willingly enough, though his face was glum.

"Dash it all, Ed, I told you we should have come sooner!" he said accusingly. "Miss Wheaton's waltzes were already taken and I nearly had to fight Naseby for the supper dance— and that's the only one I got, too!"

Wrotham shook his head sympathetically. "Poor Charles! Undoubtedly she'll tire of all those pretty fellows soon enough and see your true worth. No point rushing your fences, after all."

Ellerby agreed dubiously, making Wrotham feel like a hypocrite, for wasn't that just what he himself was doing? Instead of thinking, as he had promised himself he would do, Wrotham distracted himself from Miss Wheaton by signing the dance cards of several other young ladies, including two dances with Miss Heatherton and two with Lady Alice Gresham, hoping thereby to throw Lady Penrose off the scent. He had no mind to be subjected to her match-making again if he could help it.

The musicians struck up the first dance and Jonas led Deirdre out, determined to undo the damage done yesterday as speedily as possible. Miss Wheaton's "Dreams of July" had proved to him, beyond any doubt, that she could, indeed, compose poetry. As his wife and mentor, she could teach him to create such verse, such beauty.

"Miss Wheaton," he said, almost as soon as the dance began, "please allow me to apologize again for my behaviour yesterday. Your comments were perfectly valid and, as I had asked for honesty, I had no shadow of a right to take offence."

"I... I'm sorry too, Jonas," she replied, delighting him with her use of his Christian name. "I was perhaps more frank than was necessary. And... what thought you of my work? Please do be honest." She looked up at him expectantly, almost fearfully.

Jonas hastened to reassure her. "I must beg your pardon also for the things I said pertaining to your poetry. I see I was... quite wrong. Do you suppose," he concluded humbly, "that you could see your way clear to helping me to improve mine?"

Deirdre smiled, relieved and flattered. This was the first time anyone outside her family had seen her poetry, and though she had given him copies of two of her best poems, Mr. Flinder had every reason to be critical. However, it appeared he had liked it!

"Certainly, Jonas," she replied. "It is always a pleasure to discuss poetry with a fellow enthusiast." Her smile faltered as another thought occurred to her: what would it be like to be married to a man who hated poetry, to be never able to discuss it again?

Surely, deliberately pursuing such a course was unthinkable.

Her conflicting feelings stole much of the pleasure she should have felt at her waltz with Lord Wrotham a short time later. They also made her appear aloof and mysterious and all the more alluring, though Deirdre was of course unaware of this. Instead, she was trying to analyse precisely what it was about this man that made her breathing and heart rate accelerate so alarmingly whenever he was close to her.

"You look very serious," commented Lord Wrotham as she pondered. "What are you thinking about?"

Deirdre's eyes flew to his face in alarm. "I... ah, I was just thinking how grand this house is and— and how many people there are here, all under one roof," she managed to say, since the truth obviously would not do at all.

"Yes, in spite of the size of this ballroom, Lady Millbanke always manages to fill it beyond capacity," he replied. "Are you too warm? Would you care for a breath of air, or perhaps a glass of ratafia?" There was genuine concern in his face.

Embarrassed that he should think her so faint-spirited, Deirdre gave him a brilliant smile that made him blink as though dazzled. The idea of stepping outside into the cool night air alone with him was far too tempting to contemplate, she realized with regret. "No, my lord, I am fine. It would be a shame to miss any of my first real ball, don't you agree?"

Lord Wrotham inclined his head in assent, conscious of a

pang of disappointment. He had been hoping for a chance to speak with her privately— more privately than was possible during a waltz, at any rate—to discover more about this fascinating young lady's character. With an inaudible sigh, he realized he had received some information already; Miss Wheaton evidently preferred the glitter of a ballroom to quiet conversation.

Having told the Marquis that she felt perfectly well, Deirdre almost immediately became aware that it was uncomfortably warm in the ballroom, packed as it was with fashionable humanity. Were all balls to be like this? She hoped not, for there were apparently a great many still ahead for her this Season.

Deirdre was just gathering her courage to open the subject of poetry again —she had to discover if he really detested it— when the music ended. Mr. Barclay was there to claim her for the next set before she could leave the dance floor, and the chance for private conversation was over for the moment.

"Until later, Miss Wheaton," said Lord Wrotham with a sweeping bow, and he was gone. Rallying her smile and her energy, she commenced the cotillion with Mr. Barclay.

~

When Mr. Flinder claimed his second dance of the evening, he was, if anything, even more solicitous than he had been before. "I find I suffer every moment I am away from your side, dear Miss Wheaton," he said soulfully as he led her out to the dance. "Are you certain you will not grant me another set after supper?"

But Lady Penrose had made the seriousness of a third

dance with any one gentleman very clear to her daughters, and Deirdre had no wish to commit herself in that manner— not yet, at any rate. Would she have declined had Lord Wrotham asked the same question? Alas, she honestly didn't know.

As the strains of a country dance sounded, Mr. Flinder grimaced in disgust. He had advanced a certain sum to the orchestra leader to have a waltz played for this set, but the arrangement had either been forgotten or disregarded. "You are looking a trifle fatigued, my dear," he said suddenly to Deirdre. "Would you care to sit this one out and discuss poetry some more, instead?"

Deirdre agreed at once, for in truth, dancing was not her favourite way to spend an evening and the conversation of most of her partners had been maddeningly insipid, consisting largely of compliments to herself or of tales designed to impress her with the narrator's athletic or equestrian prowess. She had discovered a lamentable tendency in herself to compose bits of verse instead of attending strictly to their stories, though she dared to hope no one else had perceived it.

Procuring a glass of champagne for each of them, Mr. Flinder led Deirdre over to a settee placed so that its occupants could observe the dancers while resting themselves. Deirdre sipped her champagne dubiously, never having tasted it before, and set it aside after only the briefest trial.

"I recently read an interesting comparison of Sidney and Spenser," Mr. Flinder informed her, seating himself a hair closer than she would have preferred. He continued, offering, she soon perceived, the author's opinion as his own. Deirdre was obliged to disagree in some particulars, which seemed to disconcert her companion, making her wonder if he ever thought for himself or merely absorbed the opinions of others. Still, it was pleasant to cease whirling about the floor for a few moments, to discuss her favourite topic.

They had just progressed to the nature of inspiration, Mr. Flinder's theories indicating that he had read some of the same books Deirdre had, when the set ended. "I have promised the next dance to Mr. Throckwaite," she said apologetically as she rose. "Perhaps we may continue our discussion at another time."

"I shall live for that moment," Mr. Flinder promised her, bowing elaborately as the aforementioned Mr. Throckwaite came forward. Deirdre smiled uncertainly, unsure how to take Mr. Flinders's excessive gallantry, before accompanying her next partner to the floor.

Mr. Throckwaite's chosen topic was his thoroughbred hunters and his skill in riding them, in which Deirdre feigned an interest, her mind wandering back to her waltz with Lord Wrotham. To be sure, the Marquis had not flattered her unduly, nor tried to puff himself off as the best this or that in England, but his conversation had not been precisely literary, either. In spite of that, she could not say that she found him the least bit boring.

By the time Lord Wrotham claimed Deirdre for the supper dance, she had managed to subdue her contradictory emotions somewhat. She was eighteen, in London for the Season, at her very first ball, with a man she was strongly attracted to. This was surely no time to be in the doldrums! Determined to enjoy the remainder of the evening, she smiled and chatted gaily when the movements of the dance brought her and the Marquis together, and went in to supper on his arm with a heart a great deal lighter than it had been earlier in the evening.

Seated with Celeste and Lord Ellerby for supper, Deirdre had her first chance to form an opinion of this friend of Lord Wrotham's who seemed so taken with her sister, and found him to her liking. He was friendly and outspoken, but without the affectation which marred the speech of so many of the fashionable gentlemen she had met in Town thus far. Though he was clearly besotted with Celeste, he did not go so far as to fawn on her as some of her admirers did; certainly, Deirdre preferred him to the smooth-tongued Sir Malcolm.

"Well, Miss Wheaton," said Ellerby to Deirdre as she took her seat, "you and your sister seem to have taken London by storm. Enjoying your first Season?"

"So far, yes," she allowed. "Everyone has been very kind to us."

"Yes, indeed," agreed Celeste, unable to remain out of the conversation. "Why, Lord Ellerby has offered to take me to a balloon ascension tomorrow. Is that not sweet of him?" She bestowed a melting smile upon the smitten gentleman, rendering him quite speechless.

"That should be very interesting," Deirdre said. A few moments later, with sudden inspiration, she asked Lord Ellerby a question of her own. "Tell me, my lord, what think you of Lord Byron's poetry?" She had still not brought herself to reopen the subject with Lord Wrotham, but thought this might be a safe way of discovering more about his views.

"They say it's quite good, though I've read almost none of it myself," responded Ellerby readily enough. "I daresay it's the romantical stuff you ladies usually like."

"Have you never been inspired to write a verse to

anyone?" asked Celeste suggestively. More than one of her admirers, Deirdre knew, had been so moved by her beauty, which Celeste clearly found immensely flattering, though she had never subjected their offerings to Deirdre's critical eye.

"Me? Egad, no!" exclaimed Ellerby with a laugh. "But if I did," he continued quickly, at Celeste's visible disappointment, "it would be between you and me, Miss Wheaton. I'd hate to think of the dressing down I'd get were Wrotham to catch me at it!"

Deirdre glanced at the Marquis in curiosity and alarm, to see him nodding in agreement. "I pray you, Charles, if you ever feel so inclined, to spare me your efforts!" He spoke with a smile, but something in his tone told Deirdre he was perfectly serious.

"No fear of that, Ed, I assure you!" Ellerby rejoined with a laugh, apparently taking no offence.

The conversation turned to other topics, but Deirdre's pleasure in the evening had flown. It was true, then, she thought, beyond any shadow of a doubt. Lord Wrotham detested poetry. She had almost managed to convince herself that she had misinterpreted what he had said the other morning, but obviously she had not. Looking sidelong at him as he exchanged bantering comments with his friend, she found him handsomer than ever. But surely, mere good looks and a pleasant nature could not make up for a total lack of literary appreciation in a man?

As she prepared for bed a few hours later, Deirdre nearly resolved to abandon her plan to attract the Marquis. It seemed to be working all too well, especially given what her mother had said about his previous lack of interest in any lady. Her mama, in fact, seemed to consider it all but settled that he would offer for Deirdre before the Season was out.

"You do not seem to realize the significance of his dancing twice with you, Didi. And the supper dance! I do not collect that he has ever so honoured anyone before— not even Althea, whom he certainly must have admired. Why, at the few balls he attended that Season, he invariably left before supper was served. Whatever you are doing, Didi, pray continue to do so. It appears to be most effective! "

Too effective, she thought glumly. What was worse, the more she was in Lord Wrotham's company, the more willing she was to give up her poetry for the wretched man! Surely that would result in a life of misery for her, once the first bloom of love (if it *was* love) had worn off. And it would be dishonest, as well, to accept him— all the time assuming her mother was right, and that he did intend to offer for her— without revealing such an important facet of her character.

She would undoubtedly be happier, in the long run, to marry someone like Jonas Flinder, who at least admired her poetry and would encourage her to pursue it. With her help, no doubt his poetry would improve as well, and she could look forward to long evenings discussing Milton and Wordsworth to her heart's content. Why, he even looked far more like a poet than did Lord Wrotham. Yes, marriage to Jonas would surely be her wisest course. So resolved, she drifted discontentedly off to sleep.

~

Mr. Flinder came to call the next morning while the ladies

were still at breakfast, conveying his respects, via the butler, to Miss Deirdre Wheaton.

"Run along, dear, if you've finished," said Lady Penrose. "Celeste and I will join you in a moment. No doubt he wishes to discuss poetry with you yet again. I vow, I don't know what you see in the man!" Now that Lord Wrotham was a prospect, it was clear that Mr. Flinder no longer figured into her ladyship's plans for her daughter.

Deirdre rose and went to the parlour, where Jonas awaited her.

"I cannot believe my good fortune in thus seeing you alone!" he exclaimed when she entered. Coming forward, he took both of her hands in his. "I must seize the opportunity kind Fate has given me. Miss Wheaton ... Didi... I have been unable to think of anything but you these two days past. You are the woman I have always dreamed of. Will you do me the very great honour of becoming my wife?"

CHAPTER NINE

FOR SEVERAL SECONDS, DEIRDRE WAS BEREFT OF SPEECH. HOW could Jonas possibly have known of the decision she had made only the night before? He could not, of course, yet here he was, putting her resolve to the test at the first opportunity. Examining her feelings, she discovered few she had expected to feel at her first proposal of marriage. There was surprise, of course, but instead of the elation, the excitement, the joy an incipient bride should surely feel, she experienced a sinking feeling tinged with fear.

Some of this must have shown in her face, for Jonas spoke again before she was near to composing an answer. "I have caught you unawares, my dear, and must apologize. I had intended to go more slowly, to let you know my intentions and gauge your own feelings. But being confronted by your beauty, and seeing you unexpectedly alone, I dared to state my love for you boldly."

Love. That, Deirdre knew suddenly, was the problem, the one factor she had not entered into her equations the night before. Life with Jonas might hold much that was pleasant, but she did not love him. Looking at him now, with his gaudy chartreuse waistcoat and froths of lace, she somehow knew that she never would.

"Jonas, I..." she began hesitantly, hating herself for what she must say. Had she not encouraged him last night, however innocently?

"No, no, my sweet, I see that you were not prepared for this," he interrupted, stepping back and striking what was no doubt intended to be an heroic pose, but which on him looked rather silly. "I shall not press you for an answer just yet. Now that you know my feelings, my wishes, you may consider my offer at your leisure and give me your decision when you will." He stole a sideways look to see how he was affecting her and Deirdre had to smile.

"Very well, Jonas," she replied, gratefully taking the chance for delay he had offered her, even while knowing she was craven to do so. "I will consider your offer and give you my answer once I have done so."

"You... you won't take *too* long to decide, will you?" asked Jonas pleadingly, dropping his pose.

"I'll let you know within a few days, Jonas, I promise. I pray you not ask me to rush this decision."

Lady Penrose and Celeste entered the room just then, to Deirdre's relief, and the subject was perforce abandoned for the moment. Jonas greeted the other ladies before turning back to Deirdre with a literary question, only his eyes betraying what had gone before. Deirdre answered his question with alacrity, trying to forget the disturbing interlude and desirous of concealing any hint of it from her mother.

As soon as he took his leave, the ladies prepared to go out, for Lady Penrose had informed her daughters at breakfast that it was high time they made some calls of their own. They spent the morning, therefore, visiting various highly placed Society matrons and cementing the connections which were so crucial to social success in London. They ended at Mrs. Jameson's house, and found Lady Thumble already there, visiting her sister and nephew with little Theodore.

"Why, we have quite a family gathering, do we not?" exclaimed Althea as they entered. "Celeste, come help me to keep the boys from fighting over this ball and tell me about your successes; you are quite the reigning belle, I perceive!"

Celeste complied readily, seating herself without ceremony on the floor between her two nephews and taking up the ball herself. Deirdre, meanwhile, took a chair near Beata while Lady Penrose positioned herself on the sofa near the group on the floor, where she could best observe her four favourite young people in the world.

"So have you narrowed the field yet, Celeste?" asked Althea, once the boys were again happily occupied. "Who are you favouring thus far?"

Celeste glanced uncomfortably at her mother. "Well, Sir Malcolm Digby is very handsome, and most attentive, but..."

"Oh, darling, you are playing with fire there, I fear!" broke in Althea, to Lady Penrose's evident satisfaction. "Why, even since my marriage, he has flirted most outrageously with me, and I daresay with a great many others, as well. Besides, he is not particularly plump in the pocket, I hear."

"But surely, Althea, wealth should not be my prime consideration in choosing a husband?" asked Celeste.

"Oh, I would be the last one to suggest that you must completely forswear romance, sweetheart, but it *is* something to keep in mind when choosing between two or three gentlemen you are attracted to." She leaned forward, holding up the dazzling diamond-and-sapphire necklace she wore. "Isn't this lovely?" she asked. "I wheedled it out of dear Bruce only last week. Money gives a man so many more ways to show his love, you see."

Celeste eyed Althea's necklace thoughtfully before turning the discussion to other subjects.

"And what of you?" asked Beata softly of Deirdre once the others were deep in conversation. "I had no chance to speak to you last night, but I could not help but notice that Lord Wrotham took you in to supper. Does our plan appear to be working?"

"I... I suppose so," replied Deirdre, trying to smile, but Beata was not deceived for a moment.

"What, do you not care for him now that you have come to know him better? You are not obliged to accept him if he offers, you know. As long as Mama does not hear of it, that is!" she whispered teasingly.

"No, I like him quite well, actually," said Deirdre. "It is just that we seem to have so little in common, I can't help but wonder if marriage to him would be a mistake."

"Oh, fustian!" Beata dismissed her sister's concern with a wave of her hand. "How much does any woman have in common with her husband? I know next to nothing of the government matters which claim most of Mark's time, but I daresay we have as happy a marriage as you'll find anywhere, none the less." Glancing across the room, she ascertained that the others were still engrossed in the little boys' antics and lowered her voice. "The question, Didi, is whether you love him."

Deirdre sighed. "I... I'm rather afraid I do, Beata. But you haven't heard the worst yet. Lord Wrotham hates poetry!"

Beata regarded her with surprise. "Does he indeed? That seems unlikely, from what little I know of him. But if that is true—" her tone became rallying "—you are just the one to convert him. Look on it as a challenge, Didi. Don't wilt at the first set-back!"

In spite of herself, Deirdre found herself smiling at her sister's words. "There, that's better," said Beata bracingly. "After all, he must like you, if he wished to eat his supper with you last night."

At that, Althea looked up. "Yes, Didi, I noticed you at table with Lord Wrotham at Lady Millbanke's. What a triumph for you! But pray, do not set your hopes too high. He admired me greatly as well, when I was first out, but never made an offer." Her tone implied that if *her* charms had not brought the Marquis to the sticking point, Deirdre's stood little chance of doing so.

"Don't mind her," whispered Beata as soon as Althea turned away. "She was never the type to appeal to him—which means he must have more in common with you than you suppose!"

～

Upon their return to Penrose House, the Baroness and her daughters found that a number of cards and invitations had been delivered in their absence. Among the requests for their presence at various balls, routs and teas was a note from Lord Wrotham asking Miss Deirdre Wheaton to drive out with him that afternoon if she were not previously engaged. He would call at half past four.

Lady Penrose was in transports at this further evidence of the Marquis's interest in her daughter, but Deirdre viewed the invitation with mixed emotions. Beata's counsel had gone a long way towards resolving her conflict about his lordship, making her determined to at least become better acquainted with him before passing irrevocable judgement. His note, however, seemed little short of a command, with no apology for such short notice. Was he so sure of himself? The thought pricked her pride.

And, of course, there was Jonas to consider. Her talk with Beata had firmed her resolve to refuse him, though she had not mentioned his offer to her sister or anyone else. Beata's questions had caused Deirdre to examine her feelings for Lord Wrotham, however, and she had come to realize how wrong it would be to marry Jonas with no stronger emotion than friendship for him. She must tell him as soon as possible, she knew, for delay would only make it harder for her and more painful for him.

"Didi," called Lady Penrose at twenty past four, "are you not ready yet? Lord Wrotham will be here in but ten minutes!"

"I'll be down in a moment, Mama," answered Deirdre, checking her reflection one last time in the cheval glass. Her carriage dress of white cambric trimmed with violet was becoming, and the matching bonnet and parasol completed the effect, but she was not pleased. Did Lord Wrotham truly care only about her appearance? Would it not be a fitting test of his affection to appear as "herself," in one of her drab gowns, her hair pulled back in its old bun? There was not time to change now, of course, but the idea was worth considering.

~

Lord Wrotham was glad that Brooks, his valet, was up to all of the latest cravat styles, for he had never been willing to give his neckwear the concentration or practice necessary to achieve a fashionable look. It seemed such a frivolous waste of time which could be better spent improving one's mind. But if he were to properly impress Miss Wheaton of his suitableness as a potential spouse, he must conform.

For, after less than a week's acquaintance, he had decided that she was indeed his choice. He had danced and spoken with more than a dozen other unexceptionable young ladies, but none had affected him half so strongly as Deirdre Wheaton. It was not her face, precisely, nor her voice, nor the things she said that attracted him, though all of those were involved. No, there was some other quality, some underlying facet of her character that he could not quite put his finger on which drew him to her.

Whatever it was, he meant to offer for her, and thereby put this silly courtship business behind him. He hoped that after they were married she would not insist that he continue in the social whirl. He had spent a month last fall in the Lake District, where he had been fortunate enough to spend some time in conversation with both William Wordsworth and Samuel Coleridge, who lived in the area. It had been such a sublime experience that he had already formed a vague idea of settling there at some point in the future, and had purchased several acres in the district against that eventuality.

Glancing at his watch, he shook his head at such airdreams. He must make very sure of Miss Wheaton before putting such a plan before her; if she were like most fashionable young ladies, the idea of living so far from the social hub of London would be anathema to her. And he was already late for their drive this afternoon!

~

Deirdre was a bit affronted that Lord Wrotham should be late, especially given the peremptory tone of his note. When he was shown in, however, he was all apologies for his tardiness.

"Miss Wheaton, can you forgive me? I have no right to expect it, I know, but I pray you will still be so kind as to drive out with me today."

"I suppose I must, my lord," responded Deirdre with a reluctant smile. "I have nothing else to do just now; my mother saw to that!" His chuckle gave evidence that he cared no more for Lady Penrose's match-making than did she, which she found encouraging.

As they left the house, they found Lord Ellerby mounting the steps to collect Celeste for the balloon ascension. "I won't propose making it a foursome," said Lord Wrotham, "as I see we are both driving phaetons. Besides, it would hardly suit your purpose, would it, Charles?" he asked banteringly. "Good luck!"

"No more would it suit yours," Ellerby shot back with a smile. "Good luck yourself!"

Lord Wrotham appeared somewhat disconcerted by Ellerby's remark and Deirdre was hard put not to laugh. Beata had been right; they must let the men think they did the pursuing! But it seemed that Lord Wrotham did not wish the world to know he was doing it—if that were what he was doing —nor could she blame him. Look at her mother's reaction already!

Trotting along in Lord Wrotham's elegant phaeton, his groom very properly perched up behind, Deirdre could not help thinking that they must make a very attractive picture to passers-by. "Your horses go very well," she commented, feeling that some conversation was called for. Lord Wrotham had not spoken since Lord Ellerby's embarrassing riposte.

"Yes, they are not nearly the nags they look," he replied with a sudden twinkle.

Deirdre realized that her remark had not been exactly complimentary to a man of Lord Wrotham's stature and opened her mouth to apologize when she saw his expression. He was remembering his similar remark about her appearance two days earlier, and her response —she was certain of it. She began to chuckle, and he joined in readily. Their glances meeting, they dissolved into laughter and Lord Wrotham was forced to slow the horses to a walk until he had himself back under control.

"You are revenged, I think," he gasped finally, wiping his eyes. "It would seem that neither of us are expert with pretty compliments."

"I suppose not," replied Deirdre, still smiling. "But that is hardly a profound flaw in one's character, is it? I admit I would rather have genius in other areas."

"I, too," agreed the Marquis. There! He had known she was not so shallow as the other ladies he had met, and that remark proved it. They turned into the Park gates then, perforce slowing to a walk as the fashionable hour of five was approaching and the paths were choked with their usual stylish throng.

"Is there ever a time when Hyde Park is not so crowded?" asked Miss Wheaton, looking about in some dismay. "I had thought it would be nice to walk here sometime, for I walked a good deal of the time at home, but I would not care to do so in such a press, I admit."

"Early morning is best for that," replied Wrotham, pleased to discover this titbit about his companion. "I often come here then to ride alone, to be private with my thoughts. Perhaps you would care to join me one morning?"

Deirdre pinkened slightly. "But then you would not be private with your thoughts, my lord," she pointed out.

"A great sacrifice, I admit," he said with mock seriousness, "but the company should be worth it."

Her blush deepened. "There, my lord, and you said you had no skill with a compliment!"

"Even I have my rare flashes of brilliance, I suppose," he returned. After a brief pause, which the Marquis used to strengthen his resolve, he said with studied casualness, "Have you ever had opportunity to view the Lake District, Miss Wheaton? I spent some time there a few months past and found it quite... interesting." He feared it would sound pretentious to mention the slight friendship he had struck up with Mr. Wordsworth.

"Did you?" Deirdre began excitedly. She knew that several of the great living poets either resided there or visited frequently, apparently drawing inspiration from the spectacular views. It had long been a dream of hers to go one day. "I have heard that... that the scenery there is quite breathtaking," she finished rather lamely, remembering in time Lord Wrotham's aversion to poetry. Would he even have heard of Coleridge or Wordsworth?

"Yes, it is," he assured her. "I mean to go back some day." That was as close as he dared come to revealing his long-term plans at this stage. He had no wish to frighten Miss Wheaton away, especially now that he was discovering new depths to her character.

"I... I should very much like to see it myself. Do, pray, tell me about it," she prompted him.

He went on to describe the rocks and lakes in some detail, though never mentioning what had appealed most to him about his stay, and she absorbed everything he said eagerly, wishing she dared ask about the very details he was omitting.

When Lord Wrotham returned Deirdre to Penrose House a short time later, she found that Mr. Flinder was awaiting her in the drawing-room. While she had been disappointed a moment before when Lord Wrotham had declined to come in, she was now relieved; this would be a perfect opportunity to tell Jonas that she could not marry him. Celeste had not yet returned from her outing with Lord Ellerby and Lady Penrose was busy at the back of the house berating one of the maids over some misdeed, so they would have a few moments alone.

Jonas came eagerly forward to greet her, and Deirdre could not help but notice how thin, almost gaunt, he looked compared to the Marquis. And his crimson-and-yellow waist-coat was anything but flattering to his pale complexion and muddy brown hair. Quickly, she thrust such unfair physical comparisons from her mind. She must prepare to be kind. Before she could say a word, however, he burst into speech.

"Didi, did you see it?" he asked excitedly, waving a paper in his hand.

"See what?"

"The *Examiner*. It just came out. Look!" He thrust the paper under her nose. "No, no, there!"

Her eyes followed his pointing finger and she saw, in black

and white on the front page, her very own "Dreams of July"! Elation surged through her, to be quickly replaced by alarm until she scanned to the bottom and saw that the author was listed simply as *D*.

"But how...? When?" she asked dazedly, raising her eyes to Jonas's face.

"I might well ask the same!" he said accusingly. "You never told me you had sent any of your work to Mr. Hunt. I thought we were friends, Didi! I would never have known it was yours, had it not been one of the pieces you allowed me to read." His resentment was swallowed again in excitement. "You are famous, Didi! You shall be recognized as a poet, now!"

"I... I never knew he meant to print anything," she said feebly, still bemused by what had occurred. "I only wanted his opinion on whether it might be publishable. I suppose this is my answer!" She was becoming excited in her turn now.

"That explains why your name was not signed, as you did not give specific permission for the printing. But now we must tell everyone that *D* is really Miss Deirdre Wheaton," he declared. "My affianced wife!"

CHAPTER TEN

"YOUR WHAT?" GASPED DEIRDRE, SHAKEN OUT OF HER momentary euphoria.

"Yes, think of it, Didi," Jonas went on excitedly. "We shall be in great demand socially; poets always are. And of course—"

It was imperative that she stop him at once. "I never said I would marry you, Jonas," she said, more sharply than she had intended. Softening her tone somewhat, she continued, "In fact, I have thought seriously about your offer since this morning, but I fear my answer must be no. I value you greatly as a friend, but—"

"It is Wrotham, is it not?" broke in Jonas harshly, his excitement giving way to angry disappointment. "He is a better catch than I, no doubt, with his fancy title and vaunted wealth. Now that you will be famous, you may take your pick, I suppose. I would not have thought you so mercenary, Didi."

"Jonas, please..." she said, attempting to put her hand on his sleeve.

"No, I see you clearly now!" He pulled away from her as

though she scorched him. His pride clearly wounded, he struck back cruelly. "You are no different from your sister, playing off your suitors one against the other. I might have thought your muse would win out over mere wealth and position, but I see it is not so. We could have written such beautiful sonnets together, Didi—" He broke off, the sudden pain in his eyes cutting her to the quick.

He turned away abruptly. "Goodbye, Miss Wheaton. Give my compliments to your mother," he said in a muffled voice and rushed from the room.

Deirdre's legs gave way and she sank, trembling, onto the divan. She had been so certain refusing Jonas was the right thing to do... but was it? Could he have been right, that she was putting worldly considerations —not wealth, of course, but the marquis's appearance and her physical response to him— ahead of her art? Had she made a terrible mistake turning Jonas away?

As her head cleared, she honestly thought not. In fact, she realized that Jonas had tried to force her decision with his sudden declaration —and why? Because her poetry had been published? Perhaps love was not his sole motivation for wishing to marry her, either. Someone in her position could no doubt do a great deal for an aspiring poet, particularly as his wife.

Her position? she thought suddenly. Just what was her position? She had been published, yes, but anonymously. Did she dare make her authorship of "Dreams of July" (one of her better poems, to be sure) public? What would her mother say? And... what would Lord Wrotham think?

The sound of the front door roused her from her thoughts, and when Celeste and Lord Ellerby entered the room a moment later she sat composedly embroidering, the incriminating copy of the *Examiner* safely bestowed in the bottom of her work bag.

"Oh, Didi, it was the grandest thing! You should have seen it, really you should! You'd have written a poem about it for certain!" exclaimed Celeste on seeing her sister, making Deirdre start guiltily and glance at Lord Ellerby.

"The balloon rose so majestically into the sky, and the two men in its basket did not look in the least afraid," Celeste went on heedlessly, "though I vow I would be positively *petrified* to sail up to such heights! Would not you, Charles?" She turned for verification to Lord Ellerby, who had somehow become Charles during the course of the outing.

"Petrified is putting it much too strong, m'dear," he protested, unwilling to appear in any way cowardly before his divine Celeste. "I daresay it would be quite a memorable experience, not to mention educational."

Celeste looked at him adoringly. "No, I suppose *you* would not be frightened in the least. How ever could I think it?"

They chattered on for a few minutes, relating the entire scene for Deirdre's benefit, before Lady Penrose bustled in to greet Lord Ellerby warmly and to apologize for her absence upon his arrival.

"I caught Molly, that new maid, actually trying to polish the bannisters with lard instead of beeswax, simply because she could not find any!" She shook her head at such incompetence. "But that is neither here nor there. Will you stay to dinner, my lord?" she asked Ellerby hopefully.

"Afraid I can't, m'lady," he replied with obviously sincere regret. "I've already agreed to meet some friends at White's. But Cel... Miss Wheaton tells me you're to go to the theatre tonight. Might I perhaps look in on your box during the inter-mission?"

This was agreed upon and he took his leave. Immediately, Lady Penrose pounced on Celeste with eager questions about her afternoon with Lord Ellerby; she had not missed his near slip, nor the fact that her daughter had referred to him by his Christian name when making her farewells.

"Yes, I enjoyed our outing very much," replied Celeste to her mother's queries. "He is most attentive, and very pleasant."

"And more the true gentleman than a certain person you were favouring before," added the Baroness with a significant nod.

"Sir Malcolm, you mean," replied Celeste, never one for subtleties. "Yes, I believe you are right. Besides, Sir Malcolm did not call today while we were out, nor did he dance with me but once last night, though I noticed he had two waltzes with Mary Ferguson."

"Going after easier prey, I'll warrant, with a less watchful mama," commented Lady Penrose with a sour smile. "You are well rid of that one, my dear, mark my words."

"Lord Ellerby only danced with you once as well, did he not?" asked Deirdre cautiously. "You are not favouring him only for his wealth, are you, Celeste?"

"He wanted another dance with me, only he arrived too late," replied Celeste with a toss of her head. "It is not at all the same thing. And no, I truly like Charles, Didi, so you must not say such things. Wealth is important, of course," she said with a quick glance at her mother, "but I would not marry only for that. Charles adores me, which I find very pleasant."

Clearly uncomfortable with such self-examination, Celeste

quickly changed the subject. "What of you and your Lord Wrotham? Did you enjoy your drive with him?"

Deirdre gave her sister a half smile. "We are not even on a first name basis as you and your Charles are, so he is hardly 'my' Lord Wrotham," she replied, her new secret suddenly weighing on her conscience. Was he ever likely to be that now? In sudden decision, she pulled the *Examiner* from her work bag. "Mama, Celeste, I... I have something to show you."

"An article, my dear?" asked Lady Penrose, taking the proffered paper. "I rarely read this paper, I must admit, as it tends more to politics and literary matters than to the important social news."

"Not... not an article, Mama," Deirdre corrected her. "A sonnet. There."

Her mother read it through, a baffled frown furrowing her brow. "It is very nice, I suppose, Didi, but you know I rarely read poetry and am no fit critic. What did you wish to ask me about it?"

Celeste, however, had been watching her sister's face. "It is yours, Didi, is it not? You have had a poem published in a paper, and never told us! What a good joke!" She reached across to take the paper from her mother.

"Is Celeste right, Didi? Is this one of your poems?" asked Lady Penrose in astonishment. Deirdre nodded almost fearfully.

"But your name is not on it!" complained Celeste, who had not yet even read the sonnet. "Why is that?"

"Because your sister is not completely lost to a sense of what is proper," stated Lady Penrose firmly. "She was quite right to refrain from having her name bandied about in the papers." At Deirdre's crestfallen expression, her tone softened. "I am very proud of you, of course, my dear, and I am certain your father will be vastly pleased, but you do understand that it would be best to keep this in the family, do you not?"

"Why, that seems shabby beyond anything!" protested Celeste. "I should think she should want to tell the world. Don't you, Didi?"

"Not... not if Mama thinks I ought not to, I suppose," replied Deirdre, half-rebellious, but on the whole rather relieved to have the matter taken out of her hands.

"Most assuredly, I think you ought not to," said Lady Penrose. "I am sorry, Deirdre, but young ladies of fashion simply don't go writing things for the public papers. It would be... vulgar."

"It is not as though I were on the newspaper staff, Mama, or working for pay," Deirdre reminded her, though without much hope.

"I am perfectly aware of that, Didi, but the fact remains that there are those in Society who would seek to make a scandal out of it, regardless. Lord Wrotham's apparent interest in you is bound to create a few enemies out of mere jealousy. And he would no doubt be less inclined to offer for you were this to become common knowledge. Studiousness is rarely seen as an asset in a young lady, you know."

That much was no doubt true, Deirdre had to admit. It would be bad enough to have him discover that she wrote poetry at all, but for him to find that she was one of the poets in the paper he so despised ...

"I will not bruit it about, Mama, I promise," she said quietly. "I may tell Beata, though, may I not?"

"Certainly," agreed Lady Penrose. "I see no point in trying

to keep it from the family. I daresay she will even be pleased about it."

Deirdre excused herself at that point, feeling that she could not bear any more of her mother's opinions just then. In her room, she sat in her favourite chair by the window and stared blindly out at the street scene below her.

No matter what Lady Penrose said, it was quite an accomplishment to have had her poetry published by Mr. Hunt, something she had every right to be proud of. But if no one knew that it was hers, how could she ever become the celebrated poet she had always dreamed of being? And if they did know, Lord Wrotham would no doubt wish never to have anything to do with her again. She would keep her secret for now, she decided —after all, she had promised her mother as much —but not forever. Someday, perhaps, after she had "converted" Lord Wrotham as Beata had suggested she would be able to, everyone would know that D was really Deirdre Wheaton.

But right now... At the least, she must write a letter to Faith, enclosing a copy of the front sheet of the *Examiner*. It was nice to know that there was *one* person she could count on to be delighted rather than embarrassed at her accomplishment.

⁓

Scowling and muttering, Jonas Flinder paid off the driver of the hack which had carried him to Graham's on St. James's Street, his preferred haunt. He felt like the Wedding-Guest in Coleridge's *Rime of the Ancient Mariner*, having had his hopes and high spirits so suddenly drowned in tragedy. How could

Didi throw him off like that? Had she not all but promised to be his wife?

Jonas had rehearsed Deirdre's joyous acceptance of his suit so many times that he had come to believe it accomplished; her refusal had sent the elaborate castle he had built in the air crashing down about his ears. He felt betrayed, cheated, tricked, in a way a less imaginative man would not have been. Surely, all the world must be laughing at him at this moment!

Glancing dully around the club, he saw but one table, in a dimly lit corner, unoccupied. He made his way to it, ordering a bottle of port from a passing waiter. Though not ordinarily a heavy drinker, he felt that he needed it just then. He settled himself comfortably and proceeded to go through the wine at a pace which would have done credit to any of the four-or five-bottle gentlemen in Town.

Jonas had not quite lost the use of his wits when Mr. Gates, who he vaguely recalled was some connection of Lord Wrotham's, joined him at the table. Jonas scowled blearily across at the newcomer.

"Whatsit you want?" he demanded belligerently. "T'rub salt in my wounds? Go congratulate your kinsman instead!"

Since their encounter in the Park two days ago, when he had detected an uncommon interest, even jealousy, in Lord Wrotham's manner, Myron Gates had suspected that Miss Deirdre Wheaton was the lady chosen to deprive him of his inheritance. He had made it his business since then to discover everything he could about the young lady, including the fact that Mr. Jonas Flinder was her most persistent suitor.

His sources included gossiping dandies, who derived their amusement from watching the antics of other members of the ton at various functions, as well as casual acquaintances and even servants. He had been relieved to discover that the marquis had apparently made her no offer as yet, and he intended to do all in his power to prevent him from doing so.

Myron had come to Graham's quite by chance but, upon seeing Mr. Flinder engaged with a bottle, decided to join him with the purpose of influencing him to forestall his cousin in proposing to Miss Wheaton. Jonas's first words, therefore, caused him no small amount of alarm.

"My dear Mr. Flinder— Jonas, is it not?— whatever can you mean?" he managed to ask with feigned disinterest. "Have you had some sort of setback?"

Flinder squinted at the figure before him and nodded gloomily. "A setback," he repeated. "That's putting it mildly." He went on to relate what had happened, too far into his cups to recognize the impropriety of thus unburdening himself to a virtual stranger. With the aid of his fanciful mind, he embell-ished the facts in the telling to such a degree as to imply that he had been jilted practically at the altar.

"Why, Mr. Flinder," said Myron in exaggerated astonish-ment when Jonas had finished. "Surely you will not take her refusal so tamely as this? Where is your spirit, man? You must show her who is master. Make her marry you!" A cowardly man himself, he understood that Flinder would need substan-tial bolstering if he were to be goaded into action.

"A fine buck like you..." He shook his head in apparent disbelief. "The girl must be mad. You must bring her to her senses, else she will regret it her whole life." He continued in this vein until Flinder began to feel quite full of himself, ready to take on the world.

"You're right, my friend," he said finally, rising unsteadily and throwing enough coins on the table to pay for the spirits he and Myron had consumed over the past hour. "I can't allow her to throw away a prize like myself. 'Twill be for her own good."

He clapped Myron on the shoulder and bade him farewell before venturing out into the street to look rheumily about for a hackney. What he needed right now, he decided as a cab pulled up, was someone who could truly appreciate his many fine qualities. He directed the driver to take him to Drusilla's apartment in Seven Dials.

∾

Lord Wrotham sat sipping brandy and reading the newspapers at White's, where he awaited Lord Ellerby and two other gentlemen for dinner and their weekly game of whist. Looking up, he saw Ellerby and Sir George Fenton coming towards him and greeted them with a smile.

"Well met, gentlemen! And where is Manfred?"

"Couldn't make it," said Sir George with a shrug. "Appears he promised to squire some chit for the evening and couldn't cry off."

Charles snorted. "If I'd known that, I'd have stayed at Lady Penrose's for dinner. Always knew Manfred was a fribble."

"We can always play at vingt-et-un or hazard," suggested Wrotham easily. "At any rate, the food here is good. Shall we order our dinners?" He waved over one of the waiters hovering in the room.

"Have to excuse me, Ed, I'm afraid," said Sir George apologetically. "When Manfred told me earlier he wasn't coming, I promised Phoebe I'd be by. And she can be the very devil when I'm late!"

"Wish he'd told *me* earlier!" said Charles sourly. "Well, if you ain't joining us, you'd best be off to your doxy. I daresay Ed and I will go on well enough." The thought of that missed dinner with Celeste, with whom he had made remarkable progress that afternoon, smarted.

Sir George touched his forehead mockingly and took himself off and Ellerby settled himself gloomily across from Wrotham. "Can't trust those fellows for tuppence," he grumbled. "Nodcocks! We'd best find ourselves another pair for whist, Ed."

"Oh, George and Manfred are well enough. Don't tell me you set that much store by our weekly game, Charles. This would only be the third time we'd played."

Charles smiled reluctantly as Wrotham began folding up his papers in preparation for the dinner which would soon be arriving. "That's better. I daresay... half a moment, I missed this!" The Marquis bent his attention to one of the pages before him for a few moments, then whistled softly.

"I take back everything I said about Hunt the other day," he declared. "Have a look at this, Charles." He passed the Examiner across the table.

"Come now, Ed, you know poetry ain't my thing," Ellerby protested when he saw what Wrotham pointed to. He scanned it none the less. "It reads well, I'll admit, though. Real vivid picture it paints; sort of puts you right in it, eh?" He handed the paper back.

"It does that," replied Wrotham, reading through the sonnet again. "And more. Remarkable. One of the best pieces I've read in a long while. See how the metre flows, with no artificial feel, as you so often find? And it has a marvellous complexity of meaning. First, there's—"

"I pray you, Ed, no more!" exclaimed Ellerby, holding up his hands in surrender. "I said I liked it, is that not enough? Spare me the scholarly critique!"

"Very well," said Wrotham with a sigh. "I wish I had *one* friend in England who could appreciate such things," he continued with a wink at Charles. "Scholars are more plentiful on the Continent, I find."

He paused, looking at the paper again consideringly. "By *D*, it says here. Wouldn't you know it? Glennis had no qualms about signing his name to that piece of trash the other day, but here we have a real gem and the author doesn't own to it." He shook his head. "I'd like to meet this chap. Now *he's* likely to be someone I could discuss things with on a higher level. He has a real gift."

CHAPTER ELEVEN

BRIGHT AND EARLY A FEW MORNINGS LATER, ATTIRED IN ONE of the simple walking dresses she had worn before her "transformation," Deirdre left Penrose House for Hyde Park. Neither her mother nor her sister were yet awake, but Lady Penrose had not objected to her plan when Deirdre had put it to her the night before, so long as she brought along either a maid or a groom for propriety's sake.

Since she had no desire for conversation during her walk, Deirdre had decided to ride to the Park, with Granby, the groom, in attendance. Once there, she continued on foot, the groom following at a discreet distance with the horses. It seemed a deuced silly waste of the man's time and energy, she thought as she walked along, but she dared not defy her mother on such a point.

Deirdre's thoughts had been in such a turmoil since Jonas had pointed out her sonnet in the *Examiner* that she scarcely knew what she did or said half of the time. She felt she needed this walk to clear her mind, to decide what direction she wished her life to take.

At the theatre Saturday night, Lord Wrotham had stopped briefly at their box along with Lord Ellerby, but he had seemed preoccupied and left after only a few minutes. In spite of her own preoccupation, the pang of disappointment she had felt when he departed had reinforced her decision to proceed with her plan and to win the Marquis over to a love of poetry later, if that were possible. Beata had seemed to think it was. First, however, she must captivate him, so that he would be willing to listen to anything she said, however much it might go against his inclinations.

She nodded firmly at this decision, feeling better already, and wishing she had not hurried so in getting ready that morning. Suppose Lord Wrotham were to see her like this, in her dowdy gown and with her hair pulled back in such a simple style? Before, she had thought to test him in that way, but now it seemed too risky. His good opinion meant too much to her. She looked about self-consciously and, as though her very thoughts had conjured him, she became aware at that moment of the Marquis walking towards her on the path.

Deirdre's first impulse to turn and avoid Lord Wrotham was thwarted when he hailed her.

"Good morning, Miss Wheaton," he called. "You have taken my advice, I see."

As he came closer, Deirdre could detect no revulsion, or even surprise, at her less-than-fashionable appearance. Could it be that he did not mind? The thought emboldened her to reply. "Yes, I have sorely missed my morning walks since coming to London. But I thought you said it was your practice to *ride* in the Park of a morning."

Wrotham grinned sheepishly. "And so it is," he admitted. "My horse is tied yonder, in that copse. I dismounted when I saw you. Perhaps your groom would be so kind as to untie the poor beast and lead him along with the others?"

Granby nodded before Deirdre could relay the request and quickly went to retrieve the Marquis's horse. "Am I interrupting your ride, my lord, or do you also enjoy walking?" Deirdre felt compelled to ask.

"I enjoy both, but I prefer walking with a companion to riding alone," he replied with a smile which made her heart beat uncomfortably fast. "And what of you, Miss Wheaton? Do I interrupt what was intended to be a solitary walk?"

"No... well, yes it was intended so, but I have already done the thinking I wished to do," she said confusedly, blushing slightly. "You are perfectly welcome to join me now," she concluded quickly.

He looked down at her with an enigmatic smile which made her wonder if he had guessed what it was she had needed to think about. "Thank you," he said quietly.

They walked on in silence for a few moments. Deirdre looked about her in appreciation. Here, one could see spring at work as one could not elsewhere in the stony city of London. The grass was already green and flowers graced the tips of the branches in a small grove up ahead. Rounding a curve in the path, Deirdre saw a little rose garden, with one perfect red bloom on the bush nearest them and an equally perfect white one on the bush beside it.

"'The roses fearfully on thorns did stand, One blushing shame, another white despair,' " she quoted softly without thinking. The words of that Shakespearean sonnet fit the scene so well.

Lord Wrotham gazed at her in evident surprise, but just as he was about to speak, Deirdre shook herself and realized with alarm what she had said. "Are not the roses lovely, my lord?" she asked brightly, hoping that he had not noticed her slip.

"They are indeed, Miss Wheaton. As lovely as yourself," he added, for the sole purpose of seeing her blush. They continued on for a few paces, and then he asked abruptly, "Tell me, Miss Wheaton, do you ever read the *Examiner*?"

That sonnet he had read on Saturday —and reread many times since —had continued to haunt him. If this girl knew poetry, there was a chance she might know some poets as well, and he hoped that she might have a clue as to that particular one's identity. He had half formed a plan of assisting the man financially, if he were in need of it, but first he must discover who he was. So far, the few discreet enquiries he had made in literary circles had disclosed nothing.

Deirdre, however, had suddenly gone rather pale. "The *Examiner*?" she repeated in a high, unnatural voice. "Is... is that a book?"

"No, a literary newspaper," he replied, looking at her curiously. What ailed the girl? "It prints poetry occasionally, as I think I mentioned once before."

She remembered vividly the one other time he had mentioned the *Examiner*: the time he had scorned the poetry in its pages as drivel! Fearful that she would hear her own piece subjected to the same scathing judgement, something she couldn't possibly endure from this man who meant so much to her, Deirdre answered quickly, in the same artificial tone.

"Poetry? Well, no wonder I never heard of it! My father is a scholar, my lord, but the rest of us are hardly literary." She stared fixedly into the distance as she spoke, and so missed the sudden disappointment in Lord Wrotham's eyes.

"I see. Well, never mind then," he said flatly. Then, with an animation that sounded oddly forced, "It looks as though it will be a splendid day, does it not?"

Deirdre responded absently and barely knew what they discussed for the few remaining minutes of their walk. She was busy cursing herself for her cowardice. Surely, the Marquis had given her the perfect opening to reveal her love of poetry, and to determine whether she might be able to strike some chord of response in him? And she had thrown it away in her panic! Would she ever be able to summon the courage to tell him the truth now?

It was still early enough when Deirdre returned to Penrose House that she was able to change into one of her new day dresses and have her hair becomingly styled before descending to breakfast with her mother and sister. As Mrs. Jagels was often fully occupied with Celeste's hair and even that of Lady Penrose, who had discovered that her skills were superior to those of Mims, Marie had persuaded the hairdresser to teach her one or two of Deirdre's favourite styles and was now fairly competent with them.

Deirdre was preoccupied throughout the morning, barely attending to Lady Penrose's comments during breakfast or those of their various callers afterwards. She was reliving the scene in the Park that morning and wondering if, just perhaps, she could have been mistaken about Lord Wrotham. Perhaps he had been about to praise her sonnet rather than condemn it.

What she wouldn't have given to hear that! It could just as easily be, however, that his comment about the *Examiner* had nothing whatever to do with her poem and that she had taken fright at naught.

She absently agreed to drive out with Mr. Barclay that afternoon as he left with the last of their callers, something she never would have done had she been properly attending. The usual hour for morning calls had passed when Mr. Leigh Hunt was announced a few minutes later. Lady Penrose greeted him cordially, but it was apparent to Deirdre that her mother had no notion of who he was. As he advanced towards her, however, Deirdre had to restrain the urge to rise and curtsy to this celebrated essayist, critic, poet and playwright, publisher of the *Examiner* itself!

"Your servant, my lady," responded Mr. Hunt to the Baroness's greeting. "Might I know which of your fair daughters is Miss Deirdre Wheaton?"

Lady Penrose's eyebrows rose at his phrasing, but she introduced him to both of her daughters as etiquette required. Thanking her, he seated himself near Deirdre with a reassuring smile.

"Miss Wheaton, you must forgive me for not calling sooner. As you gave no hint of your connections in your letter, I had some little difficulty in locating you."

"Letter?" echoed Lady Penrose in astonishment. "Deirdre, do you mean to say you have... just who are you sir?" she demanded of their guest, her head tilting back dangerously as she regarded him down the length of her patrician nose.

Deirdre cringed. Mr. Hunt was a veritable giant among the literati of London, but it hardly surprised her that her mother would not know this, as Lady Penrose did not move in such circles herself.

"Mama, this is Mr. Leigh Hunt, the publisher of the *Examiner*," she interposed quickly. Then, as her mother still looked blank, she added, "You must know, the paper which printed my sonnet."

Lady Penrose's brow cleared as her suspicions were laid to rest. "Ah!" she said. "A literary gentleman. Now I understand." Deirdre knew that to her mind, a scholarly gentleman was by definition harmless.

"I hope you do not mind terribly that I printed your poem without consulting you, Miss Wheaton," continued Mr. Hunt, now that his identity had been settled. "I needed a piece for that issue, and I had no time— the pressures of business, I'm certain you understand." Deirdre nodded uncertainly. "To be perfectly frank, Miss Wheaton, from the tone of your letter I rather feared that you might refuse permission, so I took this step on my own, though of course I did not publish your name without your authorization."

"I... I am very pleased that you found my sonnet worthy of your paper, Mr. Hunt," said Deirdre hesitantly. "Really, all I had expected was your advice on whether or not my collection might be publishable. I did not presume—"

"No," he broke in, "I am the one who presumed. And I must tell you, Miss Wheaton, that the response to your sonnet has been extremely favourable thus far. I have received numerous letters about it, all demanding to know who the new poet is. That is why I am here."

"You have not told everyone?" exclaimed Lady Penrose in alarm. "I would not have my daughter branded a bluestocking, Mr. Hunt. Surely you can understand."

"Yes, my lady, of course, of course," he said quickly, throwing a sympathetic glance Deirdre's way. "Though surely 'branded' is rather a strong term? Now that I know who Miss Deirdre Wheaton is, how exalted her connections—" he half bowed in the Baroness's direction "—I can see why her anonymity must be preserved. *D* I signed her name and *D* she shall remain, in my paper, at least."

Lady Penrose sighed in relief, but Deirdre wasn't sure if she were more relieved or disappointed. To be famous... And he had said that her sonnet was well received! She was eager to hear more on that topic, but Mr. Hunt spoke before she could think of a discreet way to enquire.

"Miss Wheaton, I have come to ask your permission to publish more of your poetry— anonymously, of course! " he added, with a glance at Lady Penrose. "Also, to ask if you have any works which you have not yet shown me. I am very impressed with what I have seen thus far and would like to encourage you to have a volume of your poetry published, as a book. I have received more than one offer to undertake that endeavour, based solely on your 'Dreams of July.'"

"Would... would that be done anonymously as well?" asked Deirdre shakily, scarcely daring to believe her ears.

"That would be your decision," he replied. "Of course, your patrons may well demand to know your identity before advancing any sums of money..."

"Out of the question!" declared Lady Penrose. "You are suggesting that my daughter *sell* her poetry? How vulgar!"

Mr. Hunt looked slightly taken aback. "Well, er, you may get back to me on that matter, Miss Wheaton. About any other works...?"

"I've written only one or two poems since arriving in

Town," said Deirdre, still half-dazed. "One is fairly short, but the other—" She broke off suddenly, remembering the long poem she had written the day she had discovered Lord Wrotham's aversion to poetry. She had only read it over once, but she knew that it was by far the best thing she had ever written.

"Whatever you can send, I'll be glad to see," Mr. Hunt assured her. "If I might include your 'Nightingale's Song' in next week's edition?" He glanced from Deirdre to her mother.

"As long as her name is not printed, I have no objection, I suppose," said Lady Penrose stiffly. Deirdre could not suppress a smile.

"I'll bid you good day then, ladies. Pray consider the idea of a published collection, Miss Wheaton," were his parting words as he bowed himself out of the room.

"Well!" exclaimed Lady Penrose when he had gone. "I hope you will not let this go to your head, miss! Still, I suppose I must write to tell your father about all of this. He will undoubtedly be pleased," she predicted sourly. "Just remember if you will, Didi, that gentlemen do not care for literary females. It is the surest way to frighten them off." Having imparted this pearl of wisdom, she rose to consult the house-keeper about that evening's dinner menu.

～

Lord Wrotham watched Deirdre and her groom ride away down the path towards the Park gate, a frown furrowing his brow. He simply could not understand Miss Wheaton. At one moment she quoted lines from one of Shakespeare's more obscure sonnets, and the next she spoke as if poetry was something she had scarcely heard of. Her father was a scholar, she had said; perhaps the lines were simply something she had heard him say, which had remained in her mind.

For she was not dull-witted, of that Wrotham was certain. Even when discussing something as inconsequential as the weather, her words were well chosen, reflecting a keen intelligence. If it were possible, he would almost have thought she seemed *afraid* to admit to a knowledge of poetry. But of course, that was absurd.

With an effort, he thrust all thoughts of Miss Deirdre Wheaton from his mind and, immediately and unbidden, the words of that haunting sonnet "Dreams of July" arose to take their place. His desire to meet the author returned in full force and he made a sudden decision. He would go to the office of the *Examiner* and ask Mr. Hunt himself who had penned it. The fellow, whoever he was, must be encouraged in his art; Wrotham merely desired to ascertain that he would be.

Riding in the direction of the business district later that day, Wrotham realized that a large part of his enthusiasm to discover the unknown poet's identity stemmed from a hope of becoming acquainted with him, of cultivating another literary friend in London. He cautioned himself that he was like to be disappointed, as he had been before. Take Byron, for example. Reading the man's poetry, Wrotham had thought he would like him instantly —until he got to know him. Lord Byron's dissipated, even wanton lifestyle had soon killed all desire in Wrotham to befriend him. This fellow might well be cut from the same cloth.

"Still, it cannot hurt to meet him," he told himself. Charles was the best of good fellows, but Wrotham often found himself longing for a deeper level of conversation than Lord

Ellerby could provide him. He was acquainted with many of London's literary gentlemen, of course, but could call none of them close friends.

Wrotham strode purposefully into the offices of the *Examiner*, therefore, and asked the young man who greeted him whether Mr. Hunt were in. "You may tell him that the Marquis of Wrotham desires to speak to him." Wrotham rarely made use of the influence his rank accorded him, but the young man had looked disposed to argue and he had no wish to wrangle with him.

"Certainly, my lord, right away, my lord," replied the clerk, his eyes widening respectfully. Nobility were not unheard of in this office, but their visits were rare, and usually by appointment.

Mr. Hunt was apparently not so awed by the importance of his visitor as his underling, for he left the Marquis kicking his heels for some ten minutes before inviting him into his inner office. It did not occur to Wrotham to take offence, however: Hunt's genius, particularly as a critic, placed him on equal footing with a peer of the realm, at least in the mind of so literary a man as Wrotham.

"Pray be seated, my lord," said Mr. Hunt, gesturing to the most comfortable-looking chair in the office. "I have no sherry to offer you, but perhaps you would care for a brandy?"

"Thank you, no," declined the Marquis politely. "I'll not take up any more of your time than is strictly necessary. I know you are a busy man, and I would not wish to interfere in any way with the production of your excellent paper."

Hunt bowed his head in acknowledgement of the praise and Wrotham continued.

"I require some information from you, Mr. Hunt. Specifically, I wish to know the identity of the poet who wrote that most exceptional sonnet, 'Dreams of July,' the one who merely signed himself D. "

Mr. Hunt smiled. "I fear a great many people share that wish, my lord. I have been inundated by requests for our anonymous new poet's name. Quite a talent, don't you think?"

"Indubitably," agreed Lord Wrotham. "I believe he has the potential to surpass Byron. Who is he, Mr. Hunt?" he asked bluntly. "I might be willing to subsidize his career in part, so you will admit I have a reason for asking."

The publisher's smile broadened. "Alas, you are also not the first to make that offer, my lord. Unfortunately, I must tell you that I spoke to the young... man only this morning and he is absolutely resolved upon maintaining his secrecy, as is his family, and I cannot fault her, er, his reason. Money does not appear to be a particular object with them. I am sorry, my lord. D must remain unknown to the world, at least for the present."

CHAPTER TWELVE

LORD WROTHAM RODE SLOWLY AWAY FROM THE *EXAMINER* office. He could not fault Mr. Hunt; indeed, his respect for the man was increased by his refusal to be swayed by rank to break his word. The Marquis would simply have to work on the few clues supplied him during the interview. He reviewed them carefully.

Mr. Hunt's slip, from which he had quickly recovered, told Wrotham that the mysterious poet was in all likelihood a female. The reference to family, in addition, implied that she might very well be a lady of Quality, perhaps a married one whose husband did not wish his wife's name made public. Either her first or last name likely began with the letter *D*. Finally, Hunt had spoken to her only that morning, so it had to be someone currently residing in London.

Wrotham considered the various ladies he knew of who might fit those circumstances. Lady Doncastle, perhaps? Her husband would certainly not wish his wife known for scintillating verse, as he was such a dullard himself. Or what about

Mrs. Hervey? Wasn't her first name Dorothea? She was known to be a bit of a bluestocking, besides.

Finally, he shook his head in resignation. He simply had too little to go on; *D* might be one of a dozen or more married ladies. The initial might even have been chosen to throw people off the scent. Besides, if the poet were a lady— and maybe Hunt was so shrewd that the slip had been deliberate —his hopes of a friendship would likely come to naught anyway.

Checking his watch, he saw that it was half past four. Miss Wheaton would surely distract his mind from the matter. If he fetched his phaeton at once, he could be at Penrose House before five to take her driving. His mood considerably lightened by this decision, he turned his horse and set it into a brisk trot.

~

Deirdre would have forgotten her engagement to drive out with Mr. Barclay if her mother had not reminded her, so flustered was she by Mr. Hunt's visit that morning. She had spent much of the afternoon with Beata, who alone of her relatives in London could be relied upon to understand her conflicting feelings. When she returned to Penrose House it was past four, but the time had been well spent, for her mind was more settled than it had been for days.

"Gracious, Didi!" exclaimed Lady Penrose when she entered the drawing-room. "You are still in your morning dress. Is that what you plan to wear to the Park? By the bye, I can't think why you should want to encourage that spindle-shanked Mr. Barclay when Lord Wrotham is so much better a catch."

Deirdre choked on a laugh at her mother's description of Mr. Barclay. "How uncharitable, Mama," she exclaimed. "I merely agreed to drive in the Park with him. It seemed uncivil to refuse, when I had no other engagement." In truth, she scarcely remembered her conversation with the man, so overshadowed had it been by her next visitor. Not that Mr. Barclay was particularly memorable, even at the best of times. "I shall change at once."

Upon her return, properly clad in a lilac carriage dress, Deirdre was dismayed to find Lord Wrotham awaiting her.

"I had hoped to take you driving again, Miss Wheaton," he said regretfully, "but your mother informs me you are already engaged. Perhaps another day?"

Deirdre felt a sharp pang of disappointment. *Drat Mr. Barclay*, she thought almost involuntarily. Whyever had she agreed to go with him? "Perhaps," was all she said, however. Perhaps it would be as well for Lord Wrotham to understand that she was not at his beck and call.

The same thought apparently occurred to the Marquis, for he said, "I see I must plan further ahead with such a popular lady as yourself, Miss Wheaton. I shall hope to engage you for another drive within the week."

She inclined her head regally, mindful of the advice Beata had just given her. "That would be pleasant, my lord," she said coolly, and was rewarded by a searching look from his lordship. Keep him wondering, was what her sister had advised. He seemed to be doing just that, no doubt wondering too, who it was she had a prior engagement with.

"Bid you good day then, Miss Wheaton, ladies," he said with an all-encompassing bow.

Unfortunately, Mr. Barclay arrived just before Lord Wrotham was out of the house, announcing loudly to the butler that he was come to take Miss Wheaton driving. Deirdre, eyeing Mr. Barclay's thinning blond hair, spreading waistline and, yes, spindle shanks, in some dismay, thought it extremely unlikely that Lord Wrotham would be jealous.

To make matters worse, it became apparent during the drive that Mr. Barclay had discovered, most likely from Celeste, Deirdre's affinity for poetry. He therefore tried to impress her with his own knowledge, which was obviously quite limited.

"'Shall I compare thee to a summer's day? Thou art more temperate and lovely,'" he misquoted, gazing soulfully at her face.

Deirdre refrained with difficulty from correcting him, only saying brightly, "Ah! I see you are familiar with Shakespeare's sonnets, sir." Her statement was undoubtedly an exaggeration, for not only was the quote from one of the Bard's more commonly known poems, but Mr. Barclay had reversed two of the words. Still, it seemed only kind to reward his effort to please her.

"Shakespeare?" Mr. Barclay looked alarmed. "Er, yes, of course. Quite a follower of poetry, you know." He reddened as he spoke and Deirdre realized, with a spurt of amusement, that Mr. Barclay had actually been attempting to pass the famous lines off as his own.

For the remainder of the drive, Deirdre's escort seemed afraid to say anything, beyond some rather obvious comments on the weather. That suited Deirdre quite well, as she was busily composing another sonnet. The news that her work was not only publishable but apparently in demand had fired her with a sudden enthusiasm to produce more.

By the time Deirdre returned home, she had nearly finished the new poem in her head and ran upstairs to write it down after only a cursory greeting to her mother and Celeste. That evening, she pleaded a headache rather than attend Mrs. Blakely's rout so that she could devote herself to her poetry. By the time she went to bed, her desk strongly resembled the one in her room back home in the country, with scattered notes and bits of rhyme littering its surface.

Much as she would have liked to, Deirdre realized that she could not repeat her headache excuse the next evening to avoid Lady Heatherton's musicale. Besides, several of the literary gentlemen she had already met would likely be there, and she had a desire to speak to them again with her new-found confidence. Not, of course, that she would actually tell them that "Dreams of July" was her sonnet! She knew that Lord Wrotham was to be there as well, but she was not certain whether she wished to seek him out or avoid him. At any rate, she would be attending and he could seek her out if he so desired.

Celeste was resplendent, as always, in a gown of chiffon the same blue as her eyes, trimmed in vivid pink and purple. Deirdre could not help but notice the eagerness in her sister's face as they alighted from their carriage at the Heathertons' doorstep, and wondered if Lord Ellerby had put it there. She herself was dressed with more subdued elegance in a pale green gown with matching ribbons woven through her hair, and carried herself with an assurance which had been absent only a few days ago. It was amazing what success did for one's spirits, she reflected.

Lady Heatherton, an old crony of Lady Penrose, shared the Baroness's penchant for overstated opulence, apparent by the profusion of gilt and fantastically carved accents in her home. The buffet table was lavish, the platters of food interspersed with *objets d'art* placed for effect. The order of the evening, of course, was to be music, provided by no fewer than half a dozen prominent pianists, violinists and chanteuses. A dais, therefore, had been erected at one end of the music room, with chairs arranged before it. Small alcoves would allow those more interested in eating or talking to do so without apparent rudeness to the performers.

To the delight of both the Misses Wheaton, Lord Wrotham and Lord Ellerby hurried forward almost the moment they arrived. Deirdre was too busy trying to steady the sudden pounding of her own pulse to notice the proprietary way in which Charles took her sister's arm, or the trusting, adoring gaze Celeste bestowed upon him.

"I missed you at Mrs. Blakely's last evening," said the Marquis softly as soon as the other members of the party were occupied in conversation. "I would have called this morning to see how you went on, but I have sadly neglected my business affairs of late, as my secretary constantly reminds me. Are you quite well enough to be out?"

Deirdre took a deep breath to ease the sudden constriction in her chest. "Of course, my lord. My headache was largely fictitious, I confess. I stayed home so that I might... rest." Dear God, she had almost told him the truth! Something in her longed to confide in him. The concern in his voice had been genuine; surely he cared enough for her now that he would not condemn her?

"Perhaps I should have done likewise," he said, the tension in his eyes easing. "I had a dashed dull evening there, and would have done better in my bed, I make no doubt."

The thought of Lord Wrotham in his bed was suddenly an extremely tantalizing one to Deirdre. Before she could dwell on it, however, he spoke again.

"Are you fond of music, Miss Wheaton? Several noted artists are to be performing this evening, I understand."

"Yes, I very much enjoy music, my lord," she replied, "though I fear I am sadly ignorant about it. I should like the opportunity to learn more." Music had not been an important part of the education of the Wheaton sisters; only Faith, who already showed remarkable proficiency on the pianoforte, had actively pursued the discipline.

"You must have that opportunity then," said Lord Wrotham with a smile, obviously pleased with her answer. "I spent last summer in Italy and, though I am by no means an expert, I learned much from some who are. If you would care to sit with me during the performance, I may be able to make a beginning in your instruction."

"Thank you, my lord, I should be grateful for your help." Deirdre's heart was pounding again. The Marquis apparently appreciated *some* of the arts, so surely his aversion to poetry could not be so deep-seated as she had feared. Perhaps while he instructed her in music, she could similarly enlighten him about poetry.

"Your willing servant, Miss Wheaton," said Lord Wrotham with a bow. "Now, as the performances are not to start for an hour, I shall leave you for the moment. There are others present with whom I must speak." His expression was regretful.

"I shall save a seat for you, my lord," she promised, returning his smile. She watched him make his way across the room, but a warm glow remained with her. Tearing her gaze away, she looked about and saw Robert Southey standing nearby, along with one or two lesser-known literary figures. She moved to join them.

"Miss Wheaton!" exclaimed the poet as she approached. "You have become quite the lady of fashion, I perceive." He had not seen her since the card-party at Lady Thumble's a fortnight before. "I hope you are not allowing the whirl of Society to interfere with your muse."

"She deserted me briefly, I'll admit, but she seems to have returned now," replied Deirdre. Mr. Southey then introduced her to the others in the group and they discussed poetry and literature with relish for some time.

"I trust you all saw that remarkable sonnet in the *Examiner*," remarked Mr. Scott, joining them at that moment. "London is agog to know who the anonymous *D* is, I hear."

"Hunt won't tell," Southey informed him wryly. "Sooner or later the author will come forward, though. That sort of talent refuses to stay hidden."

Deirdre had to exert enormous self-control to refrain from blurting out that the sonnet was hers. Robert Southey, Walter Scott— they had liked it! "Perhaps the poet has reason to remain anonymous," she managed to say.

"So Hunt says," replied Southey with a sigh. "As long as we are privileged to read more of his work, I suppose I can resign myself to ignorance as to his identity. He's every bit as good as young Keats, in my opinion, though his style is vastly different."

"I understand you make your home in Keswick, Mr. Southey," said Deirdre, unwilling to pursue the subject of her poem any further for fear of betraying herself. "Is the Lake District truly as inspirational as I have heard tell?" She had another reason for her question; ever since Lord Wrotham had mentioned that region and his desire to return, Deirdre had fantasized about what it would be like to live amongst its mountains, falls, and glens with him.

Her question successfully turned the subject, and Southey's descriptions of Windermere, Coniston Water and Scafell Pikes increased her longing to see them for herself. At least as enthralling was his casual recounting of various conversations he'd had about their home district with Samuel Coleridge and William Wordsworth over the years. Just when Deirdre was certain that she could feel no more awed, another poet joined the group, one she had not yet been privileged to meet, but whom she recognized at once from likenesses she had seen: Lord Byron.

Forgotten was her plan to tell him what she had thought of the second canto of his *Childe Harold*. It was enough to stand silently by and listen to the great men converse on topics dear to her heart. (She later discovered how lucky she had been to meet Byron at all, for he was fated to leave England permanently only a week or two after that evening.)

Lord Wrotham was not enjoying himself nearly so keenly. As he had last night, he made various discreet enquiries among the ton in hopes of finding a clue to the mysterious D's identity, but to no avail. He was gratified, however, to find that his high opinion of the sonnet was shared by all those whose views he respected.

The time for the performance was drawing near and he excused himself from a rather lengthy (and pointless) discussion with Lord Heatherton, realizing that he had yet to question any of the literary circle, many of whom were present tonight. Looking across to where several eminent bards stood together in conversation, he was startled to see Miss Deirdre Wheaton among them— standing right next to the debauched Lord Byron! Frowning with surprise and a tinge of annoyance, he made his way across to the group.

Nodding to Southey, Scott and others of his acquaintance, he also greeted Lord Byron more civilly than he felt inclined to before turning to Deirdre. "Shall we find our chairs, Miss Wheaton? I believe the first performance is about to begin."

Deirdre was surprised at the hint of displeasure she detected in his voice, but even more startling was the discovery that Lord Wrotham was apparently on easy terms with these celebrated poets and writers. Before she could mention it, however, he asked nearly the same question that was on her lips.

"How is it, Miss Wheaton, that you come to be acquainted with Southey, Byron and the rest? I distinctly recall you telling me only yesterday that you were not the least literary."

Again, Deirdre cursed her cowardice of the day before. "I... I was attempting to change that, my lord," she replied, trying to partially undo the damage. But then it occurred to her that it might be her very association with the poets which had displeased him. "My father would appreciate hearing anything I could tell him about such men, I know," she added cautiously. If only she knew what Wrotham was thinking!

But he was smiling now. "Just as I shall try to improve your understanding of music." He gestured to two chairs near the back, where whispered comments would be less likely to distract the performers or the other guests.

During the ensuing performance, he quietly pointed out details of composition and execution that left Deirdre greatly impressed with the scope of his knowledge. And he had claimed to be no expert! Had he truly learned all of this during one summer in Italy? She doubted it. And what of his casual greetings to Southey and the others, as if they were well known to him? Surely, that bespoke a man of literary, as well as musical, interests?

The Italian pianist was followed by a French chanteuse with a spectacular operatic voice. After her breathtaking recital a short break was announced, during which the guests were invited to partake of the refreshments spread in the adjacent dining-room. Reluctantly, Deirdre rose; she had been enjoying herself far more than she had expected to.

"Shall we see what the table has to offer?" inquired Lord Wrotham, extending his arm to her. She nodded and they strolled towards the dining-room, chatting comfortably of the performances.

"So! I was right, I see," came a peevish comment from just behind them. Deirdre swung round to find herself face to face with Jonas Flinder.

CHAPTER THIRTEEN

"MY LORD, " SAID DEIRDRE QUICKLY TO LORD WROTHAM, "MAY I join you in a moment? I need to speak privately with this gentleman." She simply had to keep Jonas and the Marquis from talking to each other. Jonas was the one person outside her family (and Mr. Hunt, of course) who knew her to be the author of "Dreams of July." His flushed countenance and bleary eyes made her suspect that he had been drinking and she was in a quake that he might blurt out the truth before she could stop him.

Lord Wrotham's quick frown was immediately replaced by a smoothly social smile. "Certainly, Miss Wheaton. I shall await you by the buffet table." He nodded coolly at Jonas, not requesting an introduction, to Deirdre's great relief, and strolled leisurely into the dining room.

"Jonas, I did not look to see you here," she said as soon as the Marquis was out of earshot. "I wish—"

"You wish I weren't here to queer your game with Wrotham, eh?" he broke in sourly. He gave her a lopsided smile which was at odds with the bitterness in his eyes. "That's evident."

"I was going to say that I wish to apologize for my abruptness the other day, and that I hoped we might still be friends," she corrected him rather tersely.

"Oh, I daresay!" replied Jonas with a high-pitched giggle. "How can you need me for a friend, when you are already thick as thieves with Southey and Byron, Miss Famous Poetess? Those high-and-mighty gentlemen won't give me the time of day."

"Shh! Jonas, keep your voice down. Of course I value your friendship. You have been drinking, have you not?" She tried unsuccessfully to pull him towards one of the alcoves.

"Not foxed yet, m'dear," he assured her, then scowled suddenly. "But if I were, it would be your fault, wouldn't it? So you've no call to be criticizing me!"

"Jonas, please!" Deirdre was becoming exasperated. There was one thing she had to discover. "Have you mentioned my poem to anyone?"

He snorted. "What, and further your ambitions, when you've blasted mine? No, you'll have to find another dupe to help you spread the word. Wrotham, perhaps."

Suddenly, his expression altered, as though he were remembering something. "Everything will change soon, though, my dear, and you'll find me as helpful as you could wish. You've tried to tear our souls asunder, Didi, but I won't let either of us suffer for it. You'll see." He nodded mysteriously.

"What... what do you mean to do?" asked Deirdre in sudden fear. He wasn't contemplating suicide, was he? She would never forgive herself for that!

"Nothing you'll regret, my sweet. Until then." He swept her a dramatic bow which almost overbalanced him, then made his way towards the exit.

No, it did not sound as though he meant to put a period to his existence, which was a relief, but just what *did* he mean? After a few seconds she shook her head. He was bosky. Perhaps he meant nothing, or would have forgotten it by morning. At least he was not spreading word of her identity as D—yet. She turned to join Lord Wrotham in the dining room, though much of her enjoyment in the evening had been spoiled.

Lord Wrotham asked no questions about her interview with Mr. Flinder, for which she was grateful, given that he must have witnessed at least a part of their confrontation. At the moment, she was too preoccupied in trying to unravel Jonas's riddling to worry as much about Lord Wrotham's apparent lack of curiosity than she might otherwise.

Deirdre had just begun to fill a plate from the sumptuous buffet when her already-divided attention was diverted further by the sight of Celeste apparently *tete-a-tete* with Sir Malcolm Digby on the far side of the room. Celeste appeared to be giggling and flirting, rapping Sir Malcolm across the knuckles with her fan as Deirdre watched. Glancing about, she saw no sign of Lord Ellerby.

"You must admit you have neglected me shamefully this week past, Sir Malcolm," Celeste was saying. She peered artfully through her lashes to see what effect she was having on the handsome baronet.

"I propose to make it up to you if you will but allow me,

my sweet one," he replied suggestively. "Let us step out onto the balcony where we can be private and I shall explain."

Celeste glanced round. Where was Charles? The only reason she had approached Sir Malcolm in the first place was in the hope of provoking the too-proper Lord Ellerby to jealousy. She knew that he cared for her, but he had never so much as tried to kiss her, as several other of her suitors had—not that she had let them, of course! If Charles were to try, however... Wait! Was that him coming in from the main hallway?

"Perhaps for a moment, Sir Malcolm," she said, flashing a bewitching smile that she hoped Charles could see. "I would not wish my mama to notice our absence," she added, in the vague hope that this would deter him from actually attempting anything scandalous. Having become accustomed to Charles, she found that Sir Malcolm frightened her a little.

She allowed the baronet to lead her through one of the open French windows, glancing back over her shoulder to where she had last seen Lord Ellerby. He was not there! Perhaps it had not been him at all, she thought in sudden panic. Then, rallying her spirits, she straightened her shoulders. Surely, she was adept enough at the art of flirting by now that she could prevent Sir Malcolm from taking any unwonted liberties without assistance.

Lord Wrotham, meanwhile, had followed the direction of Deirdre's gaze and saw Celeste and Sir Malcolm as they stepped onto the balcony. Was that little minx playing Charles false? he wondered. It would not suit him to have his friend hurt, especially since he himself had been the one to introduce the two.

As though attuned to his thoughts, Deirdre said, "Oh, dear! Do you know where Lord Ellerby might be, my lord? I—I fear I do not particularly trust Sir Malcolm to be alone with my sister."

"Nor should you," replied Lord Wrotham curtly. "Do you go to play chaperon while I fetch Ellerby. He should be informed about this, I think." As he recalled, Charles had still been in the ballroom when they had quitted it.

Deirdre regarded him uncertainly, worried as to what he might say about Celeste to Lord Ellerby, for she knew that her sister truly cared for the Earl. However, she realized the wisdom of his suggestion —more an order, actually —and hurried to follow her sister, the crowd and her skirts hampering her movement. She had just reached the French windows when two things happened.

"Sir Malcolm! I thought you wished to tell me something! " she heard Celeste say in a high, unnatural voice. At the same moment, she was brushed almost roughly aside as Lord Ellerby strode past her onto the balcony. Unable to restrain her curiosity, Deirdre peered into the darkness where Lord Ellerby was bearing down on the couple a few steps away.

"Come, my sweet," Sir Malcolm was saying as he possessed himself of both of Celeste's hands. "You'll not convince me you didn't know— what the devil?" This, as Lord Ellerby grasped his shoulder from behind and spun him round.

"Charles!" gasped Celeste in obvious relief.

"I perceive you are annoying the lady," said Ellerby almost civilly, although his voice shook with anger. "You will offer her an apology and remove yourself from her presence."

Some men might enjoy a challenge, but Sir Malcolm was apparently not of their number. Nor, it seemed, had he any enthusiasm whatever for physical violence, which appeared to be in the offing if he refused Lord Ellerby's request.

"My pardon, Miss Wheaton," he therefore said obediently. With a mocking half salute to Lord Ellerby, he walked past him and back into the dining room, no doubt to pursue some other young lady who was not so well guarded.

Deirdre ducked back into the dining room when she saw Sir Malcolm coming towards her, and therefore missed the tender scene which followed out on the balcony. Suffice to say Celeste discovered that Charles could, when sufficiently provoked, behave in a delightfully improper manner.

"I... I see you found Lord Ellerby," said Deirdre to Lord Wrotham as she joined him at the table. He had filled plates for them both.

"It was not necessary," he replied. "He had already seen your foolish sister going out the door with that scoundrel, Digby. I saw no reason to impede his pursuit."

"No wonder he got there so quickly!" exclaimed Deirdre with a laugh. "And you must not call Celeste foolish, my lord."

"Oh? Is she not?" His eyebrows were raised alarmingly, but the deep brown eyes beneath them twinkled.

"Well," said Deirdre, trying not to smile, "perhaps she is, sometimes. But you should not say so!" Despite herself, she began to chuckle and Wrotham joined in.

"Most ungentlemanly of me, I agree. Now, shall we find a place to consume our repast in peace?" Deirdre followed him back to their seats, her spirits revived by his teasing, as he had perhaps intended.

The final two performers were noticeably inferior to the

first, but Deirdre could not bring herself to be disappointed. Lord Wrotham continued to instruct her in the finer points of music, and as she listened, a ballad rose unbidden in her mind, which she promised herself to put down in writing before going to bed that night. She longed to recite it to Lord Wrotham, to hear his opinion, but she dared not. Not yet. First, she must find the courage to tell him the truth about herself, and to confess that she had deliberately misled him during their walk in the Park.

~

Myron Gates glanced up and down the street before knocking at Jonas Flinder's modest residence on the fringes of fashionable Mayfair. He hoped no one had noticed his increasingly frequent visits here, for when Flinder went through with the plan they were concocting he wanted no shadow of suspicion to fall on himself. It was possible Wrotham would call him out, if Flinder were beyond his reach.

"Bid you good day, Myron!" Jonas greeted him when he was shown into the study that also served as a parlour in the small house. Lord Mallencroft actually provided his sons a very generous allowance, but Jonas proudly claimed he had never felt the need for luxurious accommodations, preferring to live in the near-squalor which seemed to inspire so many of the artists he admired.

He kept a very respectable cellar, however, which was a large part of the attraction for Myron Gates.

As usual, the two men spoke of trivialities until they were well into their second bottle. Although heavy drinking was a fairly new pastime for Jonas Flinder, it was one to which he had taken with enthusiasm.

"Never mind the race," said Jonas suddenly, interrupting a lengthy recital wherein Myron had received an erroneous tip on which horse was likely to win. "Let me tell you what Miss Hoity-toity Didi Wheaton had to say to me t'other night."

"You spoke to her?" asked Myron in alarm. "What did you say?"

"Nothin' of cons'quence. It's what *she* said I was goin' to tell you. Now what was it?" He paused for a long moment, deep in thought. "Ah! Asked me to spread the word about her poem, that's what she did. Said she wanted to be my friend." He snorted. "She knows full well that's not what I want. Know what I think, Myron?" He leant confidentially towards the other man.

Myron bent as far as his girth would allow and was rewarded by a belch in his ear. Drawing back in distaste, he said, "Well, what is it? I can't stay much longer, I'm expected at my club."

"P'raps I'll join you," said Jonas, unaware of his crony's dismay. "Anyway, I think she was hinting that she's regretting her decision now. She wants me, Myron, I'm sure of it!" He gave his companion a bleary wink.

Myron personally thought Jonas's theory most unlikely, especially considering the fact that Wrotham was all but in her pocket, but forbore saying so. "That should make your plan all the easier then, don't you think?"

Jonas nodded sagely. "My very thought, Myron! We do think alike, do we not? At any rate, given her obviously tender feelings for me, I 'spect I can do without any ropes or gags. Wouldn't contribute to our marital bliss later, I shouldn't think.

Once she's in the coach, she'll understand it's for the best, and there'll be no trouble, no trouble at all. Thought I might bring along some wine— champagne, perhaps!— instead."

Myron decided his appointment at the club could wait. "Is that quite... prudent, Jonas, do you think? Suppose you've misjudged her? It's a long way to the border, and she might contrive to escape if she's not bound."

"Escape me? I tell you, man, she loves me! She as much as told me so! Wrotham ain't her sort at all. She left him quick enough to talk to me. You should have seen how eager she was to send him on his way!"

Myron was beginning to wish heartily he had never met Jonas Flinder, but as he had, and as he had started this scheme, it was obviously up to him to see that it was carried out correctly.

"Very well, Jonas," he said cautiously. "Tell me, how do you plan to lure her into your coach? The ball for her and her sister is less than a week away, you know, and it is high time your preparations were made. Where will you spend your first night on the road?" Even if they never achieved the border, Myron thought, if it became known they spent a night together, Miss Wheaton would be effectively ruined, and no longer a threat to his inheritance. Wrotham would never marry her after that!

~

"So you see, Beata, I believe I may have been wrong about Lord Wrotham detesting all poetry." It was two days after the musicale, and Deirdre had joined her sister for breakfast and advice. "The question is, how am I to tell him the truth now?"

"It will appear odd, I admit," said Beata. "If only you had not made a point of telling him that you were not literary. You can hardly say, 'Surprise! I am not only literary, I am the mysterious *D* that everyone is talking of.' I think you will have to build up to it gradually— throw out hints, as it were."

Deirdre thought hard for a moment, then said decisively, "I had best tell you everything, Beata. Not even Mama knows this, but Jonas Flinder made me an offer last week."

"Flinder? Oh, the poetic one you mentioned. Gracious, Didi, you did not accept him?"

"No, no, I refused him. But he did not take it well, I fear." Deirdre still felt somewhat guilty over that, though she did not know what she could have done differently.

"No doubt he'll recover," said Beata lightly. "And I can't imagine Mama would be upset, now that Wrotham is showing you such marked attention. Where is the difficulty?"

"Jonas knows that the sonnet in the *Examiner* is mine. He had already read it before it was published. He has not told anyone yet, because he thinks that is what I desire. But if he finds I am keeping it a secret, I fear he may bruit it about simply out of spite!" He had not left her on a spiteful note at Lady Heatherton's, but he had obviously been drinking heavily and Deirdre placed no reliance on anything he had said.

Beata became thoughtful in her turn. "In that case," she said at last, "I think it would be best if you told Wrotham the truth at once. He strikes me as the sort who would find it impossible to forgive deception, particularly from one he has trusted. If he discovers the truth from someone else, Lord Wrotham may very well wish to have nothing further to do with you!"

At the same moment that Deirdre was receiving this excellent advice from her sister, Lord Wrotham was striding purposefully towards Penrose House. He had stayed home last night for the sole purpose of deciding what to do about Miss Deirdre Wheaton, and had come to the conclusion that she was essential to his happiness.

Charles's news that he had been accepted by Celeste the previous night strengthened his resolve to offer for Deirdre. Celeste and Charles planned to announce their engagement at the Wheaton sisters' come-out ball the following week, and Wrotham realized that there was no particular reason he and Deirdre could not do likewise. Observing his friend's euphoria could not help but encourage such thoughts.

So now he was on his way to offer for Miss Wheaton. He had come to believe, quite apart from the physical attraction he felt for her, that they would deal very well together. In fact, he could not imagine going through life without her. She had been very attentive to his musical instruction at Lady Heatherton's the other night, and no doubt would be equally eager to learn the intricacies of the literature and poetry so dear to Lord Wrotham's heart.

His enthusiasm received a set-back when he was informed by Celeste a few moments later that her sister was from home.

"I'm sorry, my lord, but she has gone to spend the morning with Mrs. Jameson, our sister. Would you care to leave a message for her?"

"Yes. Yes, I believe I would. I'll write her a brief note if you have any writing-paper about you." He intended to ask her to walk with him in the Park early that afternoon, before the fashionable hour. The tranquil paths would be the perfect setting for a proposal, he thought.

Celeste glanced about. "There is no paper here, my lord, but Didi always keeps a prodigious amount in her desk. I'll run up and fetch some, if you'll but wait a moment." She darted up to the second floor to rummage briefly in Deirdre's writing-desk before returning with a handful of paper.

"Here you are, my lord. Will this do?"

"More than adequate, I assure you," he replied with a smile at Charles's flighty fiancée. "I did say a brief note, you know. But what is this?" Among the blank sheets he had been handed were two or three covered with writing. Looking closer, he discovered it to be a lengthy —and remarkably good —ode, tragic in nature, in which the love of poetry and the love of a man (unnamed) seemed somehow in conflict. He had only time to glance over it before Celeste reached across to take it from him.

"Oh, I'm sorry, my lord. Didi's desk is always in such disarray. I suppose this is one of her little poems. She is forever writing them."

"Is she?" asked Wrotham, an arrested look on his face.

Celeste did not notice, but prattled on, oblivious. "Oh, yes! Didi fairly lives for her poetry. Did she not tell you?"

Wrotham's expression now became extremely thoughtful. "No. I am afraid she did not."

CHAPTER FOURTEEN

"OH, DIDI, IS IT NOT THE SWEETEST THING?" CELESTE EXCLAIMED in greeting a short time later. "Charles says he wishes me to wear this sapphire necklace to mark our betrothal until he can have a ring specially made up for me. He says the stones match my eyes." She fluttered those eyes at Lord Ellerby as she spoke, fingering a necklace which was remarkably similar to one Althea had worn a week earlier. "And how did you find Beata and little Geoffrey?"

"Quite well," answered Deirdre, setting aside her pelisse. "She sends her heartfelt congratulations to you both. I must say, being betrothed seems to agree with you," she added with a smile. The lovers gazed rapturously into each other's faces in response.

Lady Penrose bustled in at that moment. "I have sent off a letter to your father and we can look to see his reply in a day or two, Celeste, so I see no reason why we may not announce your betrothal at your ball," she said, regarding the pair with satisfaction. This Season was going far more smoothly than she had hoped. Why, if Deirdre could bring Wrotham up to scratch within the week, both of her daughters would be safely engaged less than a month into the Season!

"I don't suppose there is any chance that Father will disapprove?" asked Celeste with sudden anxiety.

The Baroness gave out with what might have been called a snort in a lesser woman. "Disapprove?" If he bothered to read Lord Ellerby's name she would be surprised. "No, your father trusts my judgement in such matters implicitly. We merely need his approval so that the formalities will have been observed."

Celeste relaxed. "Oh, I nearly forgot, Didi! Lord Wrotham called while you were out."

"Oh?" Deirdre's heart beat faster, as it always seemed to do when the Marquis's name was mentioned.

"Yes, and he behaved most strangely. He said he wanted to leave a message for you, so I got him some paper from your desk. I'm afraid I accidentally caught up one of your poems along with it, and when he asked about it I said it was yours."

"Celeste!" broke in Lady Penrose severely. "You knew that we had agreed not to speak of that outside the family."

"Well, I forgot. Besides, it looks as though Lord Wrotham will soon be family anyway, does it not?"

Deirdre felt the blood leaving her face. "Which... which poem was it, Celeste?" she asked faintly.

"Oh, this one here," said Celeste, picking up the sheets from the side table where she had left them. "He only looked at it for a moment," she added defensively.

Deirdre thought that she would swoon, something she had never done in her life. "Did... did you tell him everything?"

"Of course not!" exclaimed Celeste indignantly. "Besides, he did not give me a chance. He just walked out, not even leaving the message he wanted the paper for! Now I ask you, is that not odd?"

"Deuced odd," agreed Charles, as both Deirdre and Lady Penrose seemed bereft of speech. "Never known a poem to affect Ed like that, and by Jove he reads enough of 'em!"

"He... he does?" Deirdre couldn't help asking.

"Lord, yes! Always has his nose buried in Milton or Spenser or some such thing. Quite the scholar. I know he thinks I've no culture at all, but I say, there's time enough for that sort of stuff when I'm in my declining years!"

Celeste nodded, apparently agreeing heartily with this philosophy, but Deirdre sat back, stunned. How could she have been so utterly wrong about Lord Wrotham? And what had she lost by not telling him the truth sooner? His trust, certainly. And his love? Had she ever had that? It seemed unlikely now that she would ever know.

"Oh, well, in that case, there is probably no harm done," Lady Penrose was saying complacently. "If he is a poetry lover like yourself, Didi, then he will probably be pleased rather than vexed at your having had that piece published."

"Published?" asked Charles in surprise.

"Oh, yes!" said Celeste, since obviously her mother could have no objection now to her speaking, as she herself had said it first. "Didi is quite famous. But anonymous."

Charles was looking understandably confused, so Celeste related the entire story of Deirdre's sonnet being published in the *Examiner* under the alias *D*, as well as Mr. Hunt's visit earlier in the week to procure more poems.

"So you are the mysterious *D*." Charles shook his head in smiling disbelief. "Won't Ed be flummoxed! He's been asking questions all over Town, trying to discover who the new talent is!"

Deirdre didn't know whether to laugh or cry. Lord Wrotham had liked her sonnet, he really had! She was beginning to realize that his comments, which had led her to believe that he detested all poetry, had really been indicative of his very love of its purity; his distaste (which she shared) was for seeing inept attempts at the art. His praise was high praise, indeed! But would she ever hear it from him?

Lord Wrotham was riding faster than was generally permitted in the Park, but it was yet uncrowded and he felt that the speed might help to clear his brain. He had not yet fully absorbed the amazing discovery he had made less than an hour ago.

Miss Deirdre Wheaton wrote poetry —and exceptionally good poetry at that! This was more than he had ever dared hope. As that fact finally sank in, however, two questions rose to plague him. Why had she deliberately led him to believe she knew nothing of poetry, and who the devil had that ode been written about?

Wrotham thought over every conversation he had ever had with Miss Wheaton. She had been charming, intelligent, witty; they had laughed at the same things. She had evinced qualities he would not have expected in someone with an inferior education. Yet, she had said none of the family, save her father, were literary. When had that been? Oh, yes, when he had asked whether she had seen that sonnet in the *Examiner*. He remembered now that she had acted strangely, appearing almost alarmed at his question.

A sudden suspicion flared in his mind, crystallizing quickly into certainty. "Didi fairly lives for her poetry," her sister had said. Didi ... *D*

Of course! Why had he not seen it sooner? The answer came immediately: because she had deliberately misled him. But why? He was almost certain she cared for him. The evidence was there in her eyes, in the way she spoke, in the unconscious brightening of her face when she saw him. Why, then, would she deceive him about something so important to her?

Thinking hard, he slowed his mount to a walk. He was remembering again his recent conversation with her sister, Celeste. She had seemed to regard Deirdre's poetry as something of a family joke. "One of her little poems," she had said. What torture such an attitude must be to a serious poet, as Deirdre so obviously was. For all he knew, Lady Penrose had forbidden her to mention it to anyone —and perhaps her own family was yet unaware who *D* was. Surely, then, he should not be hurt by her reluctance to confide in him, a comparative stranger, no matter how much he loved her.

That thought brought him up short again. Love her? Yes, now that he mentally said the word, he realized it was perfectly true; had been true for some time, in fact. He tried in vain to recall the exact moment, word or look when he had become ensnared, but it had happened too gradually, hidden even from himself until now.

This realization made the answer to his second question imperative: who had that ode been about? And when had she written it? He thought over the various men he had seen her with, but could remember no particular preference she had shown to any of them, save perhaps himself.

Suddenly, he recalled her private conversation with that dandified beanpole —what was his name? Flinder? —at Lady Heatherton's. He remembered hearing from someone, Southey perhaps, that the man fancied himself a poet, though his attempts were generally laughable. Could he be the one she meant?

A jealous fury rose up in him at the thought, startling him considerably; Wrotham could not recall ever having been truly jealous before. But now, the very thought of Deirdre giving herself to that... that *fribble* filled him with rage. She deserved so much better!

He put his horse back into a trot, forcing himself to think more calmly. Surely, Deirdre could see Flinder for the ineffectual fop he obviously was. She was by no means unobservant. Perhaps it was someone else, then; someone from the country. After all, he had no way of knowing that the ode he had read had been written since her arrival in London.

There was only one way he could reasonably find out, he decided abruptly. He turned his horse towards home, rapidly making plans.

∼

That afternoon a note was delivered from Lord Wrotham and Lady Penrose fairly pounced on it. "Perhaps he wishes you to drive out with him again, Didi," she said optimistically as she unfolded the paper. She had clearly not given up hope of announcing two engagements at the upcoming ball.

Deirdre held her breath as her mother read the note, and

watched in despair as the Baroness's face fell. "What... what does he say?" she forced herself to ask.

"He has left Town, and so will be unable to accompany us to Mrs. Greene's tomorrow night. He says he will attempt to return in time for our ball on Monday, however," she added with a sigh. "We can only hope that he will, I suppose. Whatever can have taken him from Town at the height of the Season?"

"Perhaps he has business on one of his estates," offered Deirdre dully, feeling certain that it was something else entirely.

"That must be it," decided Lady Penrose. "However, if he is not to return until the ball, I suppose my mention of him to your father was wasted."

"Mama! Whatever can you mean? What did you say to Father? Lord Wrotham has never implied that he means to offer for me!" Deirdre felt herself blushing at the delicious thought, even while she knew how unlikely her own actions made such an outcome.

"Pish, tush! The whole world has noticed the attention he has paid you, more than he has ever been known to do for any other female. It's almost as good as a declaration. I simply took the precaution of asking your father's approval of Wrotham in my letter about Charles and Celeste, so that if he did make you an offer before Monday we should not have to wait on the mails to make the announcement." She was obviously well pleased with her cleverness in the matter.

Deirdre wondered if her mother had been this forward when trying to snag Lord Wrotham for Althea three years earlier. If so, it went a long way to explain his reluctance to spend much time in the Baroness's presence. Deirdre herself could not help but be embarrassed by her mother's attitude, even if she had not already spoiled everything herself, with her needless deceit.

"Are we expected somewhere tonight?" she asked, as much to change the subject as because she wanted to know.

"Of course. What a silly question," replied Lady Penrose. "We are to dine with the Heathertons, as we have not got together intimately with them since our arrival in Town, and as Margaret and I are such close friends. Afterwards, we go to the Burroughs' rout. I know Lord Wrotham will not be present, but Julia Heatherton will be, and you and she have become fast friends, have you not?"

"Oh, certainly," Deirdre lied without enthusiasm. Further acquaintance had shown Miss Heatherton to be even shallower than Deirdre had first suspected, without opinions of her own and never a thought in her head beyond gossip and fashion.

Already, Deirdre felt one of her convenient headaches coming on—or perhaps she would develop a cough this time. Socializing seemed less attractive than ever without Lord Wrotham's possible presence during the evening to look forward to. She wondered again what business had taken him from Town, and whether he might possibly listen to an apology upon his return.

～

Riding north through Bedford late that afternoon, Lord Wrotham wondered for the hundredth time whether he was doing the right thing. Might he not, in effect, be taking the decision out of Deirdre's hands? Of course, it was to prevent just that that he had decided on his present course rather than approaching Miss Wheaton or, worse, her mother in Town. First, he had to discover if there were another claim on her heart. If she truly loved whoever she had written about in that tragic ode, she would surely be miserable if forced to wed elsewhere.

Again he wished he had had time to read all of the poem; perhaps, had he asked, that hen-witted Celeste would have given it to him. But no, that would not have been right. His own few attempts at poetry were intensely personal to him. No doubt Deirdre felt likewise. If he discovered what he hoped to during this excursion, there would be ample time later to read what she had written.

It was dark when he reached the border of Northampton and too late to pay a call, so he decided to put up at an inn until morning. The Golden Goose was not luxurious, but it was clean and he had no complaints. After a leisurely break-fast the next morning, Lord Wrotham rode the last few miles to his destination.

Never having had occasion to travel in this district before, the Marquis examined the countryside with interest as he approached the village of Roseton. Oak trees predominated, and the grass was lush and green, with spring wildflowers everywhere. He could well appreciate why Deirdre enjoyed her walks here. Other than the Penrose residence, there appeared to be no houses of particular note in the area, however. His hopes rose.

Lord Wrotham stopped when he reached the open gates of Rose Manor. The house spread invitingly at the end of a long, straight drive and he impatiently shook his doubts aside. This was what he had decided was best, and now that he was here he would see it through. Spurring his horse, he trotted up the drive to dismount before the oaken double doors.

"Would you tell Lord Penrose that the Marquis of Wrotham desires an audience with him?" he said in reply to the elderly butler's offer to be of assistance. The grey-haired retainer bowed him into a cool, dimly lit drawing room and went to convey the message.

Looking about him, Wrotham decided that the room must be rarely, if ever, used in Lady Penrose's absence. The Baron must either be a recluse or an invalid, neither of which boded well for his being received. After only a minute or two, however, the butler returned and gestured for the Marquis to follow him.

"Lord Penrose will see you in his study. He is in the midst of a difficult translation and fears to lose his place if he leaves it."

Wrotham wondered whether the baron had offered this explanation or if the butler felt the need of one to justify his master's odd behaviour. In any event, it perturbed him not at all, as he often received guests in his own study at home.

"Come in, come in, and shut the door behind you," commanded his host the moment the butler opened the study door. "Draughts are something to be avoided, for obvious reasons." The stoop-shouldered little man gestured around at the sheaves of paper piled upon tables, desks and chairs. "Sit down and be quiet. I'll be with you as soon as I've finished this paragraph."

Wrotham obediently sat in the only other chair in the room which was not littered with papers and waited, examining Deirdre's father with interest as he worked. He was not actually as small as he had first appeared; it was his hunched position which gave that effect. Undoubtedly, he was not so old as he looked, either, for his hair still showed many strands of gold amidst the silver.

Straightening abruptly, Lord Penrose turned bespectacled eyes of the same clear grey as Deirdre's on his guest. "Lord Wrotham, is it?" The Marquis nodded, rising and offering his hand. His host ignored it. "And what might you want?" His bushy eyebrows drew down in a forbidding frown, but Wrotham was not intimidated.

"I have come to request your daughter Deirdre's hand in marriage, my lord," he replied calmly.

CHAPTER FIFTEEN

LORD PENROSE CONTINUED TO REGARD THE MARQUIS piercingly for a moment, then his frown abruptly disappeared and he began to chuckle.

"Well, I see you're not lily-livered, at least," he remarked after he had amused himself in this way for some seconds. "Now you can tell me why you felt obliged to come all the way out here to ask me that question. My wife generally handles such things, as you must know."

Lord Wrotham decided that honesty would best serve him. "From what I know of Lady Penrose and have heard from Miss Deirdre of yourself, I thought I would be more comfortable dealing with you, sir."

The Baron gave him a twisted smile. "Not one of those social butterfly types, eh?" He nodded. "Just as well. You won't be wanting to drag Didi about to balls and such when she could be working on her poetry and other studies. She had a poem published, did you know that?" The pride in his voice was evident, and Wrotham warmed to the man even more.

"I... was able to deduce it," he replied carefully. "It is not common knowledge about Town, you know."

"Why the blazes not?" demanded his host. Then, answering his own question, "Ah, Vivian, of course. Lady Penrose, as you have observed, tends to set great store by social, rather than literary, success. In fact, I suspect she feels that one should preclude the other. That was precisely what I feared for Didi when she left for Town. But she must have heeded my advice after all."

Wrotham nodded uncertainly at this analysis before bringing Lord Penrose back to the subject at hand. "No doubt. But as to the purpose of my visit..." He held his breath, fearing to hear of some previous attachment of Deirdre's, though indeed that had been his primary reason for making this journey in the first place. If her father, or younger sisters, knew of such a partiality, they would be less likely than Lady Penrose to pressure Deirdre into the more advantageous match which he represented.

Lord Penrose waved his hand impatiently. "Yes, yes, marry the girl. No doubt you'll do better than most of the other young bucks she's encountered by now." He snorted. "Vivian seems to have shown good judgement for once, probably by accident."

Lord Wrotham's eyebrows rose questioningly.

"Lady Penrose has already written, asking my consent to the match. I sent off my reply last night. Told you she's the one who handles these things."

"But..."

Wrotham realised in time that it would be impolitic to tell Lord Penrose that he had not yet actually offered for his daughter. It seemed that Lady Penrose had wanted to be prepared, so that there would be no delay in announcing the betrothal. Surprisingly, the knowledge that he had been that transparent did not trouble him. Flinder, or whoever that ode had been about, must be no threat after all. Suddenly light-hearted, he turned back to his host with a smile.

"I hear you are a scholar, Lord Penrose. What, precisely, are you studying now?"

This successfully diverted the Baron, who was always willing to discuss his work; it was rare, however, that he found anyone equally willing to listen. He and Lord Wrotham settled into a protracted discussion of ancient documents and the discoveries and difficulties presented by their translation.

"Do I look all right, Mama?" asked Celeste as she entered the drawing-room in a vivid pink day dress which matched the roses in her cheeks. "Charles will be arriving at any moment to take me shopping for a few odds and ends I shall need for my ball tomorrow."

Lady Penrose gazed lovingly at her Celeste. "You look divine, as always, my angel," she said with satisfaction before turning a more critical eye on her other daughter, who sat silently embroidering in the corner. "But you, Didi! Why are you wearing that old gown? I vow, you look almost as dowdy as you did in the country!"

Deirdre met her mother's gaze steadily. "I am done pretending to be something that I am not," she replied quietly but firmly. "I'm sure Celeste is fashionable enough for both of us."

The Baroness frowned. "What nonsense is this? Once you

decided to dress properly, you became an instant success, nearly as much so as Celeste. Does that not prove what I have said all along?"

"That the fashionable world judges by appearance?" inquired Deirdre with a lifted brow. "Yes, I suppose it does."

"That is not precisely what I said, and well you know it," retorted Lady Penrose defensively, as some inkling of Deirdre's meaning penetrated. "There is nothing wrong, surely, in making the most of the gifts God has given you."

"No, there is not," Deirdre agreed. "That is why I have decided to publish more of my poetry, as Mr. Hunt suggested. Under my own name."

Lady Penrose was aghast. "You will do no such thing! Do you wish the world to think you nothing more than a bluestocking? No eligible gentleman will come near you!"

"I would rather be thought a bluestocking than an empty-headed lady of fashion," Deirdre informed her mother bluntly. "Any gentleman who would avoid me because I have a mind is hardly a loss, to my thinking."

Lady Penrose was uncertain how to handle her normally compliant daughter in this new mood. She remembered that her husband had urged her to allow Deirdre to make her poetry public in his last letter, but she had carefully kept that to herself. Obviously, however, she dared not appeal to him for help.

"I have only your best interests at heart, my dear," she said finally. "What will Lord Wrotham think when he returns to find you so changed?"

"*If* he returns," put in Celeste unexpectedly. "Althea did warn you, Didi," she added. "She said not to put too much stock in his attentions. He played false with her feelings three years ago. Don't let him hurt you, too, Didi."

Deirdre had heard Beata's version of that story, and knew it was not the same. No, it was her own actions, her own deceit, which had driven Lord Wrotham away. She had learned her lesson now, and would never again deny her love of poetry, or her writing of it. Nor did she see any point, now, in taking great pains with her appearance. She had not the slightest wish to entrap some brainless beau to appease her mother. The life of a spinster had begun to look rather attractive, in fact. Love was too painful.

Accordingly, when she came downstairs that evening just in time to leave for a rout at Lady Melcher's, she was wearing the plain grey gown she had worn to Althea's card-party at the beginning of the Season. Her hair was pulled back in a simple bun, for she had refused to allow Marie to dress, or even braid it.

"Honestly, Didi!" exclaimed her exasperated mother. "I have a mind to forbid you to leave the house looking like that. Where is the blue-and-white dress I asked Marie to lay out for you?"

"I decided not to wear it," said Deirdre indifferently. "But I have no objection to staying home, if you would prefer it."

Lady Penrose glowered. "If there were time, I would require you to change this instant," she said severely. "I hope you do not mean to spoil the ball tomorrow night by some such start."

"Oh, please do not!" pleaded Celeste in sudden alarm. "You *will* wear your new white-and-lavender ball gown, will you not, Didi? It will embarrass me to death if you come looking like a servant. After all," she added kindly, "it is to be your ball as well as mine. You should look your very best for it."

Deirdre could see that Celeste was truly concerned and, in spite of her own heartbreak, she had no wish to detract from her sister's happiness. "I shall not embarrass you, Celeste," she promised. "You will be able to enjoy your ball."

Celeste was apparently satisfied with this assurance, for she spoke no more on the subject.

In spite of Lady Penrose's dire predictions, no one snubbed Deirdre for her attire at the rout, though she received a few curious glances. Celeste was surrounded by admirers as always, though she clung determinedly to Lord Ellerby's arm. Deirdre's retinue had fallen off somewhat of late, as it had become apparent that Lord Wrotham favoured her, and none of her remaining admirers seemed to be present this evening.

She told herself that she did not mind, that she would only have been bored with the empty flattery of some stylish young buck, but in truth she was feeling rather forlorn. She had become accustomed to popularity. Unfortunately, none of the literary circle appeared to be present either, which left Deirdre with virtually no one to talk to.

Midway through the evening, Beata arrived and hurried to Deirdre's side as soon as she noticed her sister standing alone. "Gracious, Didi, what have you done to yourself?" was her first remark, which did not help Deirdre's flagging spirits.

"It's more what I haven't done, Beata," she replied, with a crooked attempt at a smile which unfortunately told her sister something was dreadfully wrong.

"Will you tell me about it?" she asked simply. Deirdre nodded and Beata led her to a small divan in a quiet corner. Once seated, Deirdre took a deep breath and began.

"You were right, I fear, Beata. I should never have kept my poetry a secret from Lord Wrotham." She related the story of his call in her absence and subsequent discovery of the poem she had written about him. "He left Town later that same day. He must be thoroughly disgusted with me!" she concluded. "So you see, all of our fine plans and stratagems to attract him have come to naught. Why ever did I try to be what I am not?"

Beata soothed and shushed before going over the details Deirdre had just related. "You say Lord Wrotham is a devotee of poetry after all?" she asked.

"That is what Lord Ellerby implied," said Deirdre with just the slightest sniff. She had managed, through valiant effort, not to cry.

"Perhaps there is no difficulty then," suggested Beata after a moment's thought. "You do not actually know that Wrotham's absence has anything to do with you. It is possible he called that morning simply to tell you he was going out of Town, but your exquisite verse drove it from his mind temporarily. I recommend you do not despair until you have actually seen him. Then you can fall on his neck and confess everything, begging him prettily to forgive you."

Despite herself, Deirdre giggled at Beata's words.

"That's better," said her sister bracingly. "Now, I want you to promise me you'll wear your loveliest gown for your ball tomorrow night. Beautiful clothes can do wonders for the spirits."

Deirdre had to admit to the truth of this, for her spirits during the past two days, when she had been back in her dull things, had certainly been abysmal. Besides, she had already promised Celeste. Brightening as she always did after a talk with her sensible older sister, Deirdre went to strike up a conversation with Julia Heatherton.

~

It was gone dinnertime when Lord Wrotham arrived back at Berkeley Square. He had spent an enjoyable day at Rose Manor, where he and his host had talked far into the night on various subjects, scholarly and otherwise. They had found they had much in common and enjoyed their time together immensely.

The Marquis had accepted his host's invitation to stay the night, and had been privileged to meet Deirdre's two younger sisters over a leisurely breakfast in the morning. Elise reminded him forcefully of Celeste and Lady Thumble, but the quieter Faith was charming, and eager to know all he could tell her of her Deirdre.

He smiled, remembering her delight at her favourite sister's "fame and fortune" at having a poem published. He had also been able to glean, from references Faith had made about Deirdre's letters, that his case was by no means hopeless, and his fear of a rival completely unfounded. He and Deirdre would have her often to visit them after they were married, he decided. Engaged in such happy thoughts, he was unprepared for the mournful face of Bigby, who opened the door as he mounted the steps.

"Egad, man, has there been a death in the family?" he asked in some concern. His butler was never known for his cheerful countenance, but he was looking several shades more doleful than usual.

"No, my lord. Everything is well," he replied hesitantly, which was also unusual for the man.

"The devil you say! Come, Bigby, out with it! What has you in the dismals?"

Bigby winced at his master's phrasing, but answered readily enough. "You will recall, my lord, that before you left on Friday you asked that I set Hodge to keep an eye on a certain Mr. Flinder?"

Wrotham nodded. Actually, he had all but forgotten it, pleasurably distracted as he had been by his discoveries about Deirdre and her family, but he quickly recalled his orders. "You discovered something?" he prompted the butler.

"Indeed, my lord. It would seem that your Mr. Flinder has a frequent visitor to his lodgings, one well known to your lordship."

Wrotham's heart contracted painfully. Deirdre! Was she actually carrying on an affair with that blackguard Flinder? He would never have believed it of her. He would kill the man; kill them both! "Oh?" he asked, amazing himself with the calmness of his voice.

"Yes, my lord," continued Bigby with increasing concern. He had not missed the sudden whiteness about Lord Wrotham's mouth and eyes. "It appears he is closely associated with your cousin, Mr. Myron Gates."

For a moment, Wrotham did not comprehend; when he did, his relief was so great that he felt almost lightheaded. Bigby, who had apparently braced himself for the outburst sure to follow this intelligence, seemed flabbergasted when the Marquis began to laugh.

"Myron?" he gasped after a moment. "It is *Myron* who has been visiting Mr. Flinder? That— that is most interesting, Bigby." His eyes were still dancing when he realized that his butler was regarding him as if he had gone abruptly mad. "I apologize, Bigby," he said in a more normal tone. "I have ridden all day and am famished, as well as fatigued. That was not quite the news I expected, and it took me off my guard."

"Will you be wishing to go out then, my lord?" asked Bigby, once more his unperturbable self.

"No, not tonight. Have Cook put something together for me; nothing fancy, but quick and filling. Then I believe I'll early to bed. No doubt I'll be better able to consider this... unexpected development in the morning."

"Very well, my lord." Bigby went to do the Marquis's bidding, his impassive expression masking the raging curiosity he felt. Who had his lordship expected to visit Mr. Flinder? He was destined never to know.

~

In the morning, much refreshed after a good night's sleep, Wrotham felt ready to consider the day ahead. He would call on Deirdre, of course, and finally make the offer he had intended to make last week. Only if she hesitated would he reveal that he had already called on her father and received his consent. However, he did not think she would be unwilling. According to Bigby, Flinder had not been near her for the past three days, so it seemed unlikely that any attachment lay in that direction.

The thought of Mr. Flinder brought to mind the interesting news Bigby had told him the night before. This friendship between Myron and Flinder was of fairly recent origin, and might bear looking into. Perhaps the two men had discovered a certain compatibility due to a similarity in age, style of dress and foolishness, the latter of which both no doubt possessed in abundance; but it might be something else entirely. Yes, it would definitely bear looking into.

Accordingly, after a large breakfast in his rooms, Wrotham dressed with more than his usual care, mindful that his cousin was easily intimidated by appearance, and set out to pay the inimitable Mr. Gates a call.

Normally, Lord Wrotham might have walked the distance, less than a mile, to Myron's lodgings, but instead he elected to take his crested carriage, the one with the gold trim. He rarely used that carriage, commissioned by his mother many years ago, for it was too ostentatious for his tastes; just now, however, it seemed appropriate.

The lodging house where Myron lived was more run down than he remembered. Dirty children played about an equally dirty stoop, and the door looked as though it had not been painted in years. Wrotham rapped with the tarnished brass knocker and was answered by a slovenly woman with greasy black curls. Her eyes widened at the sight of the Marquis and the elegant carriage behind him in the street, and she quickly ushered him up the stairs to Mr. Gates's room.

"Visitor for ye, Myron," she rasped, tapping at the door. "A real swell!" The door opened slowly and, with a final awed glance, the woman retreated down the stairs.

"Ed! What— what a surprise!" exclaimed Myron, palpably nervous. "Whatever can bring you to this part of Town?"

"Why, I came to call upon you, Myron, what else?" said Wrotham languidly. "May I come in?"

"Of—of course! That is... I wasn't exactly expecting you." He stepped back, allowing the Marquis to move past him into the squalid little room. It looked as though Myron had not expected visitors for months. Preferring to spend as little time as possible in such surroundings, Wrotham came directly to the point.

"Myron, I understand you and a Mr. Flinder have been quite thick of late. Would you care to elaborate for me?" He hoped, by avoiding specific questions, to glean more information than he might otherwise. He was not disappointed.

"My God! I knew you'd find out! Jonas is such a ninnyhammer, he no doubt left clues enough for a blind man to follow. I tried to talk him out of it, Ed, you must believe me!"

Lord Wrotham began to seat himself but, on closer examination of the chair's surface, reconsidered. Instead, he leaned against the wall and folded his arms, looking down his aristocratic nose at his cousin, whose paunch had begun to shake like so much jelly. "And why is he so set on this course?" he enquired, as though he knew all.

"Dash it, I don't know! I suppose he loves the girl, though half the time he talks as though he hates her instead. He's jealous of her poetry, I know, and thinks if he marries her he can pass it off as his own. But if she has half a brain in her head, she'll escape before ever they reach the border, the way he's planned it!" Wrotham straightened abruptly. This was more serious than he had suspected. "I want all the details, Myron, and I want them now. Else, I'll consider you a full accomplice."

That was more than enough for the quaking Myron, who immediately told all he knew of Flinder's contemplated abduction of Miss Wheaton: time, place, route, everything. As he absorbed the details, Wrotham began to smile.

"Myron, not a word to anyone of my visit here or of what you have told me, particularly to Flinder, and there will be twenty pounds in it for you. If Flinder calls, you are not in. Do you understand?"

He did not, but twenty pounds was twenty pounds. Myron nodded.

"Very well. You can trust me to handle it from here." Chuckling, Lord Wrotham departed, his step light.

CHAPTER SIXTEEN

PENROSE HOUSE REMINDED DEIRDRE OF A LUNATIC ASYLUM, with servants scurrying frantically about in an effort to fulfill all of Celeste's and Lady Penrose's orders in preparation for the ball to be held there that evening. Flowers and greenery had begun arriving shortly after breakfast to be placed about as decorations and just before nuncheon a remarkable miniature marble fountain was delivered for the front hall.

Celeste darted enthusiastically from room to room, hindering rather than helping the preparations and chattering non-stop. Silver was being polished and repolished at a great rate, as were the banisters and every stick of furniture in the house. When the caterers arrived with box after box of lobster patties and pastry puffs, Deirdre felt she had had all she could endure.

"Mama, would you mind terribly if I took a walk for an hour or so?" she asked the distracted Baroness. "I shall bring Marie along and be back in plenty of time to change for dinner."

"Why, I suppose not, dear," replied her mother absently. "No, no!" She rounded on a hapless footman trying unsuccessfully to place a wreath in the exact spot she had ordered. "Halfway between those two columns, there!"

Deirdre hurried up the stairs to fetch her pelisse and Marie, only to find that the latter had been pressed into service by Celeste, sewing onto her ball gown the sequins she had decided at the last minute she must have.

"I'll scarce have time to finish as it is, Miss Didi," said Marie plaintively when Deirdre told her what she had in mind. "Best you ask someone else. If only Miss Celeste had told me yesterday she wanted these sparklers, I could've done it last night, easy!" She continued stitching madly. Deirdre was half tempted to help her, but suspected she would only be in the way.

There had still been no word from Lord Wrotham; no evidence, in fact, that he had yet returned to Town. A huge corsage of lilies had arrived from Mr. Flinder, however, which rather surprised Deirdre after the way in which they had last parted. She had hoped that he would refrain from attending, but feared now that he intended to appear after all. Celeste would never forgive her if he made a scene.

Re-emerging from her room, Deirdre looked about at the bustle of activity. Celeste's voice floated up from below: "Why, Mama! These hyacinths will just match the trim on my gown. How clever of you! Charles will be charmed." Deirdre *had* to escape, if only for a few minutes. No one would notice if she went out alone, not today.

Just as she slipped out of the front door, however, a large travelling carriage pulled up before the house. Thinking it to be yet another delivery, Deirdre ducked her head to hurry past when a familiar voice called her name.

"Didi! Miss Wheaton!"

She turned back resignedly. "Yes, Jonas, what is it?" It looked as if she would not have her walk after all. Perhaps she could shake him quickly; he looked (and sounded) as though he had been drinking again.

"I come with a message from Mrs. Jameson," he replied, gaining her full attention. "She wishes to speak to you immediately on a matter of some importance. I met her shopping on Bond Street and she asked if I would be so kind as to convey you to her house, as I was already out in my carriage. Will you come?" He spoke as though reciting a rehearsed speech, but Deirdre attributed that to the alcohol in his system. At least he was not driving the coach himself.

"Why... I suppose so," she replied uncertainly, wondering what Beata could have to say to her that could not wait the few hours until the ball. Might it have something to do with Lord Wrotham? That must be it! Beata had had some word about him, and wished to pass it on to her. It did not occur to Deirdre how odd it was that Beata should have asked Mr. Flinder to bring her. Moving quickly now, she climbed into the coach as Jonas held the door for her. The coachman on top stared impassively forward.

The first thing Deirdre noticed upon entering the coach was the overpowering scent of lilies. Looking about her, she saw piles of them banked along the walls of the coach like drifts of snow. "Are you going into business as an undertaker, Jonas?" she asked as he seated himself next to her and closed the door. The coach lurched forward as he answered.

"Do you not like lilies, my darling?" he asked, gesturing

around the interior of the coach. "They are fair and sweet, as are you."

She was certain now that he was foxed. "I am not your darling, Jonas," she said severely. "And why should you have obtained them for me, if you did not know I would be riding with you until you saw Beata?"

Jonas appeared suddenly concerned. "I—I did not, of course," he stammered, as though trying to put her at ease. "I was merely delivering them for a friend."

"Oh?" asked Deirdre, thinking of the hundreds of flowers already brought in for their own ball. "Is there another ball tonight, then?"

"Ball?" repeated Jonas blankly. "Oh, of course. I mean yes, my... my friend is also having a ball tonight."

Deirdre regarded him strangely. There seemed more afoot here than a simple over-indulgence of spirits. "Jonas, I believe I would prefer to take a hack to Beata's, if you don't mind," she said decisively. "You may let me out here." She glanced out of the window as she spoke, suddenly realizing with alarm what she should have noticed sooner: they were no longer in Mayfair, but were rapidly travelling out of London.

"Where are you taking me, Jonas?" she asked sharply when he made no response to her previous request. "What on earth is going on? Take me to Beata's at once!"

"I'm rather afraid that is out of the question," said Jonas apologetically. "You see, she wouldn't be expecting you just yet."

"Just yet? You mean at all, don't you?" demanded Deirdre. "You made up that story about Beata just to get me into your coach, did you not? Have you lost your wits?" She was angry, but not yet afraid; she could not believe that Jonas meant her any harm. She would simply talk reasonably to him and persuade him to return her to Penrose House.

"You are on to me, I see," he said with a faint smile. "Yes, I have lost my wits; I lost them the moment I laid eyes on you, my beautiful Deirdre. I have come to realize that I cannot live without you, and that you would be desperately unhappy without me. Therefore, I have decided to do what is best for us both. We shall arrive in Scotland in a few days, where we can be married. Are you not happy, my sweet?"

Deirdre's mouth dropped open at Jonas's revelation. "Married?" she repeated in a strangled voice.

"Of course," he replied, smiling. "I know you were not yourself when you refused me. You could not help but be happy with me, someone who shares your devotion to poetry. That must be obvious."

She looked at him incredulously. Had he actually deluded himself to this extent? He seemed truly to expect her to be pleased at her abduction. If he were mad, as appeared likely, there was no telling what he might do if she shattered his illusions too abruptly. Perhaps it would be safest to play along for the moment, at least until she knew exactly what he planned.

"Where... where do you intend us to spend the night, Jonas?" she asked carefully. "Surely you do not expect me to stay unaccompanied with you at some inn before we are wed?"

He sighed. "I feared you would see it that way, but we have little alternative. I have arranged for separate rooms at the Silver Swan, but that is the best I can do. Does it matter so much, when we will be spending our lives together?" he asked wistfully.

Deirdre attempted a smile. "The scent of these lilies is

rather... potent, Jonas," she said, changing the subject. "Might we open the windows a bit?"

He seemed to see nothing unusual in her request and did as she bid. Deirdre was now able to see that they were already out of London, presumably on the Great North Road to Scotland. How long would it be before someone at home noticed that she was missing? Remembering the confusion there, she knew that neither her mother nor Celeste was likely to look for her before dinner. By then, they would be miles ahead of any pursuit. She would just have to effect her own rescue, she decided.

"Would you care for some champagne, to celebrate our escape from the prosaic, mundane world?" asked Jonas at that moment, producing a rather warm bottle from beneath the cushions.

"No, thank you," said Deirdre with ill-concealed distaste. "But you go right ahead, if you wish."

Jonas hesitated for only a moment before doing just that. No doubt this abduction business was more unsettling than he had expected it to be, and he felt the need for more fortification. He opened the bottle with some difficulty, narrowly missing his own eye with the cork as it popped. After drinking nearly half the bottle in silence, he became suddenly talkative again.

"I have written a poem just for you, my darling," he announced importantly. "Would you care to hear it?"

"If I must," said Deirdre resignedly. Her resolve to play along with him was rapidly evaporating. She simply had to escape soon!

Jonas pulled a folded paper from his pocket and smoothed it carefully before reading: "Miss Deirdre is the fairest in the land; I long to be the one to win her hand." Deirdre winced but said nothing and he continued: "I'll show her all the joys of paradise; and if she likes it, I shall do it twice."

At this point, Deirdre was seized by a sudden fit of coughing, which (thankfully) made Jonas stop in concern. She took her time recovering, but at length he was satisfied that she was all right. He lifted the paper again but, before he could read any more, Deirdre cried out in one last attempt to distract him from such a painful employment.

"What was that?" she exclaimed.

"What? I hear nothing," replied Jonas peevishly. "Really, my dear, you are not contributing to the romantic mood at all!"

As if conjured by her words, there came at that moment the sound of rapid hooves behind them. Jonas craned his neck to look back, and as he did a shot was fired. The startled horses broke into a canter, causing Jonas to hit his head on the top of the window as he recoiled.

"A highwayman!" he gasped, turning very white. Opening the little door in the roof of the carriage he called up to the coachman, "Faster! Faster!"

"Jonas, don't be a fool!" cried Deirdre. "We cannot possibly outrun him. We must stop and give him whatever he wants. If we anger him, he may well shoot your poor coachman!" Already, she was wondering if this could be her chance of escape. Jonas would be so shaken, she might even be able to prevail on him to return her himself.

Jonas, however, appeared not to have heard her. He was curled into a ball of misery on the seat beside her, as though expecting death at any moment. Another pistol shot rang out. Deirdre gave Jonas an exasperated glance before leaning forward to speak to the coachman herself. Before she could do so, however, the coach gave a sickening lurch and tilted to the left, throwing her against Jonas. Lilies flew everywhere. With a grinding, crunching noise, the vehicle shuddered to a halt.

A moment later, the door was wrenched open from outside and a rough voice said, "And now, me fine swells, ye will stand and deliver!"

Jonas appeared incapable of speech or movement, cowering as far away from the door as was possible in the small space.

The highwayman seemed to fill the entire opening, his bulk blocking the remaining light of the lingering sunset. He gestured with one gleaming pistol and growled, "C'mon, c'mon! Out wi' ye!" Jonas merely whimpered.

Deirdre regarded her erstwhile abductor with as much disgust as did the highwayman. Had she known Jonas was this faint-hearted, she would have forced him to free her miles ago! "What is it you want?" she asked the man outside.

She could not see his face, masked as it was, and with the fading light behind him, but she heard a faint chuckle. "That's better!" he said. "Hoy, there, me dandy," he called past her to Jonas. "You goin' to let yer doxy show ye up?"

Jonas stirred at that. "Miss Wheaton is a lady!" he said faintly. "Pray, treat her as such." His gallantry expended, Jonas huddled back into a trembling mound.

"A leddy, is't?" asked the highwayman. "Ye may be worth me trouble after all! I reckon some swell or papa would pay a pretty penny to get a gentry mort like this'n back! Climb on out, me leddy, and le' me have a look at you." He flipped down the steps of the coach.

Deirdre did as she was bid. Lifting her skirts, she managed to clamber out of the coach. She impatiently brushed at the lilies clinging to her hair and dress, to stand defiantly before the highwayman. Although she found the situation far from pleasant, if the brute intended holding her for ransom, she reasoned, he would probably refrain from harming her. At any rate, anything would be better than being forced to marry Jonas! Glancing back into the coach, she marvelled that she had briefly considered becoming his wife.

"You, too, me fine hero," he called to Jonas, thrusting his pistol menacingly into the coach. "Let's see what ye have in yer pockets!" When Jonas still hesitated, he added, "I can just as well empty them with ye dead, ye know."

At that, Jonas scrambled out of the coach to stand trembling beside Deirdre. "I—I haven't much, I'm afraid," he stammered, turning his pockets out to reveal a few coins and a ten-pound note.

The highwayman seized the proffered money, then pushed Jonas back towards the coach with a booted foot. "That'll do. I reckon the real haul is yer sister here. Ye'll be hearing from me on how to get her back. If yer papa has no more gumption than you, this should set me up as an honest man for life!" With a guttural laugh, he grasped Deirdre's arm with a grimy paw and pulled her to his horse. Throwing her across its withers with no more regard than he would show a sack of flour, he mounted behind her and kicked it into a fast canter up the Great North Road.

Jonas rounded on the coachman as soon as they were out of sight. "Why the devil did you run us into the ditch?" he demanded. "And why didn't you do something other than sit there like a stone?"

The man stammered out an explanation, but Jonas did not wait to hear it. The enormity of what had just happened struck him anew and he began to tremble again. He climbed back into the coach to comfort himself with the remainder of the champagne.

CHAPTER SEVENTEEN

LORD WROTHAM LEFT HIS COUSIN'S LODGINGS IN GOOD spirits. He had realized, very early in Myron's recitation of Mr. Flinder's abduction plans, that Deirdre was likely to be in no danger whatsoever.

This being the case, it had occurred to him that it would be most effective if he were to wait until Flinder had actually kidnapped her and to overtake them on the road, playing the role of her knight in shining armour. What more romantic setting for a proposal of marriage? The only risk he foresaw was that she might contrive to escape on her own before his daring rescue; therefore, he did not wish to wait too long.

The abduction was scheduled for later that afternoon, so Wrotham ate a leisurely nuncheon with Lord Ellerby before returning home to change into an appropriate riding costume. He rarely wore capes, but on this occasion he decided to don for effect the one caped riding cloak he possessed. He also brought along a brace of pistols against the unlikely chance that it would be necessary to persuade Mr. Flinder to release his captive. If the enterprising Jonas resembled his crony Myron in courage, it was more probable that the mere sight of a pistol would cause him to faint dead away.

Regarding himself in the mirror, Wrotham decided that he looked quite the swashbuckler. Any lady who wrote poetry as assiduously as did Deirdre could not help but appreciate the romantic image he evinced. Arching a dark eyebrow at his reflection, he swept out of the room with a flourish, fully aware that he was behaving foolishly. The logical thing to have done, of course, would have been to warn Miss Wheaton so that the abduction could never take place at all. But playing the hero was something he had never had opportunity to do and could not quite resist on this occasion.

Bigby regarded the Marquis in some surprise when he descended in his unusual attire and requested his horse be brought round. It was as well the pistols were hidden under his coat, reflected Wrotham. Mounting a moment later, he directed his horse towards the Great North Road at a brisk trot. They should be less than a mile ahead of him, he thought, which should allow him to overtake Flinder's coach within the hour.

He was surprised, therefore, when nearly two hours passed without a sign of the bright red travelling coach Myron had described. How on earth could they have got so far ahead? Only if he feared pursuit would Flinder travel at such a pace; if Myron had betrayed his plan, he would lose far more than the twenty pounds promised him!

The afternoon was deepening to dusk when Wrotham spotted a coach on the side of the road up ahead, just at the near side of Finchley Common; as he drew closer, he saw that its two far wheels were in the ditch, causing it to lean at a precarious angle. It was red.

Alarmed, he put his horse into a canter and quickly drew even with the coach. The rear axle appeared to be broken. As he reined in, a liveried servant, obviously the coachman, came round from the other side.

"What has happened here?" rapped out Wrotham sharply. "Is anyone hurt? Where is Miss Wheaton?" At his words, a white face showed at the coach window. "Who... who is that?" asked a quavering voice. "Lord Wrotham? Is that you? Thank God!" Jonas Flinder pushed open the door and struggled shakily out of the coach, crushed lilies trailing from his clothing.

Wrotham barely spared him a glance, but looked past him into the dark interior of the coach. "Miss Wheaton? Are you all right?" he called anxiously.

Flinder was shaking his head. "She's not here. The rogue took her with him!" He appeared on the verge of collapse.

"Who took her? Took her where?" demanded Wrotham. His alarm was increasing.

"The highwayman. We were held up," stammered Flinder. Wrotham feared the man would faint before getting his story out, so he helped him to sit on the coach steps, which were down. After a few deep breaths, Flinder went on. "I hadn't much money, nor any valuables, so he took Didi! Said something about a ransom to pay for his trouble."

"And you simply let him take her?" asked Wrotham incredulously. "What manner of man are you?"

"Dash it all, he had a pistol. He fired over us twice." Jonas began to tremble again at the memory.

"Twice?" echoed Wrotham. "You fool! He had discharged

two pistols then. It is unlikely he had a third, or time to reload. You allowed him to take Miss Wheaton at the point of an empty pistol!" He was tempted to fire on Flinder himself for such ignorant cowardice.

It was apparent that Jonas had not thought of that. "An empty... damnation! You may be right. But not necessarily," he added defensively. "It is possible—"

Wrotham waited to hear no excuses. Not now. "Which way did they go?" he broke in.

"North. Same direction we were travelling. Say, how do you come to be here at all?" asked Jonas as the reality of the situation penetrated. "Were you pursuing us?"

"I was," he replied shortly, cursing himself for his blasted heroics. If he had followed the logical course, Deirdre would be safe at home now.

"But how—"

"There's no time for that. Describe to me exactly how Miss Wheaton and the highwayman were dressed, the colour of his horse, everything. I must try to catch them up." It looked as though he would have to play the hero in earnest, after all.

Deirdre tried to keep her wits as she was bounced, head down, on the highwayman's horse. Surely he did not mean to take her far in this manner! She had always understood that gentlemen of the high-toby generally kept hide-outs near the scenes of their crimes. She certainly hoped it was true.

Sure enough, after only a few minutes the highwayman turned his horse off the road onto a smaller track and slowed it to a brisk walk. Jogging along in her awkward position,

Deirdre was amazed to find a poem, in the form of an heroic epic, forming in her mind. She gave herself over to it, deciding that she would be better off composing than concentrating on the discomforts of her journey.

She had progressed a fair way into the epic poem when they stopped abruptly in front of a tumbledown structure which looked as if it might once have been an inn. The highwayman dismounted and dragged her roughly from the horse, pushing her before him through the dark, doorless front entrance of the building. An ancient sign, its wording long ago obliterated by the elements, swung above it. Though Deirdre was not yet bound or gagged, escape seemed unlikely at the moment. She decided therefore to attempt reasoning with her captor. Perhaps she could persuade him to let her go.

"You would no doubt be better employed in holding up another coach," she told him without preamble. "I cannot think that you will receive much in the way of ransom for me."

"Eh?" He turned to her in evident surprise that she should speak at all rather than simply swoon at her plight. "Why's that?"

"The man you kidnapped me from just now," she explained calmly, "was taking me to Gretna Green."

The burly rogue squinted at her. "Never say a sweet piece like yerself was thinkin' to marry sech a gutless cove!" He snorted in derision.

"It was not precisely my idea, no," she admitted. "Nevertheless, my reputation is doubtless ruined now and neither my mother nor anyone else is likely to think me worth redeeming." As she said the words, the truth of them struck home and she felt tears welling up. Lord Wrotham would certainly want nothing to do with her now! His face came clear before her mind's eye and she bade it a sorrowful farewell.

The brute before her appeared deep in thought, his mouth half-open with the effort. "That's as may be," he said after a moment. "Still, a wench like you should be worth a pretty penny, even if your gentry folk won't pay. I know other sorts as would be willing to pay real handsome to sample the wares of a leddy like yerself." He laughed coarsely.

Deirdre felt a chill pervade her as his meaning penetrated. She measured the distance to the door with her eyes, but the highwayman seemed to read her thoughts.

"No, no, me leddy, can't have ye runnin' out on me!" He grasped her arms and pulled them behind her, tying her wrists together with a cord he produced from somewhere on his person. "I'd try ye out meself, but it'd lower yer value. Besides, Polly will be here any minute, and she'd have somethin' to say to that!" He chuckled to himself.

Deirdre tried to take some comfort from the fact that another female would be with her shortly, but escape had now become paramount in her thoughts. Would Jonas come after her once he'd recovered from his fright? It seemed unlikely in the extreme. She had thought anything would be better than being forced to marry him, but now she was forced to reconsider.

Her thoughts went again to Lord Wrotham, and again she fought against the tears pricking behind her eyes. If only... But her captor was pushing her ahead of him again, towards a flight of rickety steps at the rear of the building. She guessed that he must have his quarters somewhere at the back, where no light would be visible from outside. She stumbled over the first step and the ruffian grasped her round the waist to set her back on her feet. His arm remained about her, and his hand began to travel along her body.

Deirdre pulled away from him sharply, suddenly more afraid than she had yet been. This was such a lonely place! When would that Polly arrive? Chuckling, the highwayman grasped her again.

"There's some fun I can have wi' ye that won't spoil ye for ransom nor market, me leddy. Relax and ye might find ye like old Ned better than ye think!"

Deirdre was gathering her breath to scream, though she knew not who could possibly hear her, when another voice snapped across the darkened room like a whip.

"You will release the lady at once if you do not want a pistol ball in your puny brain," came the crisp command. It was Lord Wrotham.

~

After getting as much information as possible from Jonas Flinder (which wasn't much, as he had been too frightened to observe anything clearly), Wrotham had spurred his horse into a gallop along the Great North Road. The thought of what might happen to Deirdre as a result of his intentional delay goaded him like a white-hot brand. His desire to appear heroic in her eyes, his ridiculous, uncharacteristic wish for romance, had brought this pass about. If she were harmed as a result, he would never forgive himself.

After a few moments he slowed his horse to a brisk trot. It was unlikely, he realized, that a highwayman would remain on the main road for long after abducting a lady of quality. He would no doubt seek shelter from prying eyes as quickly as possible. Wrotham began to search for any path or track, any sign that a horse might have turned aside into the underbrush.

Several times he stopped to examine a break in the trees, but each time it turned out to be a false path, leading nowhere. He was about to despair when he saw, faint but unmistakable even in the fading light, a narrow rutted trail leading off to the left. Following it, he found that it continued on, and he dismounted to examine the ground more closely. There were several imprints of hooves, apparently of fairly recent origin, although he could not be certain of that. It was enough to merit further investigation, however. Praying that Deirdre's captor had stayed on the track, Wrotham remounted and urged his horse to a brisk pace.

Night had nearly fallen when he noticed the looming shape of an apparently deserted building off to one side of the path as it curved back towards the north. He almost passed it by, but his attention was caught by a shadow moving under the trees that grew hard against the walls of the house. Looking more closely, he saw that it was a horse, tethered to a low branch. Quickly, he dismounted and put one hand to his own mount's nose to discourage it from whinnying to the other animal, which mercifully remained silent.

Tying his horse next to the roan which Jonas had described, Wrotham stealthily made his way to the front entrance of the derelict inn. Pulling a pistol from beneath his cloak, he approached from the side, out of sight from the broken windows. As he reached the yawning doorway, he heard a voice speaking inside. Peering cautiously round the corner, he saw Deirdre, his beloved Deirdre, in the grasp of a great, uncouth brute who was apparently attempting to thrust his vile attentions upon her.

Forcing himself to remain calm, Wrotham took careful aim with his pistol before speaking. When the highwayman looked up at his words, it was to see the gleaming black barrel pointed squarely between his eyes.

"At once," Wrotham added as the man froze in shock. The gun did not waver.

With a curse, Ned thrust Deirdre away from him, before turning to dart through the doorway of a back room with an agility surprising in so large a man. Deirdre, not surprisingly, collapsed on the floor. Wrotham hurried forward to kneel at her side. Lifting her head, he searched her face concernedly.

"Deirdre, are you all right?" he asked anxiously. "If that monster harmed you..."

Though she appeared about to swoon, at his words she managed to rally. "I—I'm fine," she answered with a wan smile. "How did you find me?"

Guilt smote Wrotham again as he remembered how she came to be in this predicament. "Flinder told me which way you'd gone," he said. How could he tell her that it had been in his power to prevent all of this, had he wished?

"Had you not better go after that villain?" Deirdre interrupted his thoughts. "He spoke of a woman coming here soon, and he may well have other cohorts, for aught we know."

Reluctantly, Wrotham left her to look into the room where the highwayman had disappeared. It was empty, and a back door leading outside was standing open. He returned quickly to Deirdre's side.

"It appears that our host has abandoned us," he said as lightly as he could. "As I have no intention of leaving you here while I pursue him, I recommend that we leave this charming spot before he returns with reinforcements. Can you walk?"

She nodded. Wrotham helped Deirdre to her feet and slowly led her out to where his horse was tethered. The highwayman's beast was gone, and Wrotham gave silent thanks that the man had not stolen his own mount as well. Carefully, as though she were made of glass, he lifted Deirdre onto its back before mounting behind her. He kept one arm tightly about her waist as he set the horse into a walk back towards the Great North Road.

"How did you know to come after Jonas?" Deirdre asked presently, once the old inn had been left behind.

Wrotham cleared his throat uncomfortably before answering. "I... ah, I had word of his plan from my cousin, Myron Gates. It seems they were somehow in this together."

"Mr. Gates? I remember him from the Park. He and Jonas know each other?"

"So it would seem." Lord Wrotham reached up to loosen his neckcloth, which suddenly felt unaccountably tight. "Miss Wheaton, I fear I have a confession to make," he said.

"You called me Deirdre before, my lord," she reminded him. "You . . . you may continue to do so if you wish." Then, after a pause, "I have a confession of my own, you know, though it comes a bit late, I fear."

Wrotham nodded. "Ah, yes, your poetry. I wish you had told me, but I doubt not you had good cause to keep it to yourself. However, I fear that my crime is a shade more serious."

Deirdre looked up at him curiously, craning her neck to do so. "Crime, my lord?" she queried doubtfully.

"If you are to be Deirdre, you may call me by my Christian name as well," he said irrelevantly, delaying the inevitable. "It is Edison, Ed to my friends." Deliberately avoiding her eye, he bent more attention than was strictly necessary on the path ahead.

"Crime, perhaps, is too strong a word," he admitted when she continued to regard him in silence. "But not by far. Miss Wheaton... Deirdre... I discovered Mr. Flinder's plot to abduct you quite early today, and had ample time to prevent it. I did not do so, but chose to play the hero instead, coming after you once the abduction had occurred. So you see, it is completely my fault that you were subjected to this disagreeable experience." He said it tonelessly, refusing to coerce her forgiveness by so much as a look. He did not deserve it.

"Play the hero?" Deirdre echoed. The lightness of her tone startled Wrotham into looking at her. She was smiling. "Do you mean to say you did this to impress me?"

Wrotham swallowed convulsively, suddenly feeling foolish. "I... I suppose so," he admitted. "I deduced from your poetry that you shared the feminine penchant for romance and thought—"

"And thought, what could be more romantic than rescuing the fair maiden from her abductor?" Deirdre finished for him with a chuckle. "Somehow, I cannot find it in my heart to condemn you for that."

The horse came to an abrupt halt. "Then you will forgive me?" Lord Wrotham looked full into her eyes.

Deirdre felt her heart in her throat, beating more forcefully than it had during any of her recent alarming experiences. "How can I not?" she asked shakily. "What lady would not forgive her knight errant?"

Wrotham crushed her to him, heedless of the sidling horse beneath them. His lips sought hers and they met in a timeless kiss that swept away all need for explanations. At length, becoming aware again of their surroundings, they parted reluctantly.

"This is not precisely the setting I had in mind for this question, Deirdre, but will you do me the very great honour of becoming my wife?"

Deirdre thought her heart would overflow with happiness. "Yes, Ed, I will."

Wrotham tightened his grasp and would have kissed her again, but at that moment the horse shied at some small animal in the underbrush and nearly pitched both of them to the ground. The embrace changed from loving to frantic until they had regained their balance.

Laughing, Wrotham said, "I suppose any further physical evidence of my affection will have to wait until we reach Town. Which reminds me," he added, pulling out his pocketwatch and scrutinizing it in the near darkness. "You have a ball to attend, do you not? And if I am not mistaken, I have been invited as well."

Deirdre's chuckle ended in a sudden gasp. "Oh! Mother and Celeste must be nigh frantic with worry by now! I had not even thought of it till now! You are right, my... Ed," she amended with a shy smile. "We must return at once."

"Hold tight, then," advised Wrotham, gripping her firmly with one hand while controlling the reins with the other. He kicked the horse into a brisk trot.

"I wonder what Mama is doing about my disappearance," Deirdre wondered aloud as they reached the highway and turned southward.

CHAPTER EIGHTEEN

LADY PENROSE WAS AT HER WITS' END. MIMS HAD BEEN putting the finishing touches to her costume when Celeste tapped on her door to ask where Deirdre was.

"I was going to ask Mrs. Jagels to dress her hair first, Mama, so that she could take her time with mine afterwards, but she is not in her chamber. Now that I think on it, I have not seen her all afternoon, though I rather thought she must be working on her poetry in private, as she often does."

The Baroness cast back in her mind, trying to recall the last time she herself had seen Deirdre. She snapped her fingers. "I remember!" she exclaimed. "Didi asked if she might go for a walk, while we were so put about with the decorating earlier. I said she might, so long as she took Marie; but that was nigh on two and a half hours ago!"

"Marie did not go with her, Mama, for she is this moment adding a third flounce to my gown. I suppose I may as well have Mrs. Jagels do my hair first, as Didi is not back to have hers dressed." Celeste turned to go, the question of Deirdre's whereabouts forgotten in the face of more important matters.

"But where can she be?" Lady Penrose called after her in some dismay. "If she truly went out unaccompanied, there is no knowing what might have happened."

"Oh, doubtless she went walking as she said, Mama, and lost track of time as she always does at home," responded Celeste unconcernedly. She clearly had no suspicion of the pitfalls London had to offer an unescorted young lady.

But Lady Penrose did. "I shall send Peters to search for her at once," she said decisively, ringing the bell.

An hour later there was still no sign of Deirdre, and the dinner guests were due to arrive at any moment. Peters had returned after fruitlessly combing the Park and the streets surrounding Mount Street. A query sent to Beata was answered in the negative: Mrs. Jameson had not seen Deirdre at all that day. Lady Penrose knew not what other course to pursue.

When Lord Ellerby arrived a moment later, ahead of the other guests, Celeste poured the story out to him, confident that he would have some idea which had not yet occurred to them. His only suggestion, however, was that they consult Lord Wrotham on the matter at once.

"He's the very man to deal with a crisis of this sort, if you ask me," he said to his fiancée and her anxious mother. "Besides, he has more than a passing interest in the matter, I should say."

"But he is out of Town, is he not?" asked Lady Penrose in surprise. After days with no word from the Marquis, she had come regretfully to share Celeste's view that his interests had turned elsewhere. Charles's last remark, however, caused her flagging hopes to rise again.

"No, he returned last night. I dined with him this afternoon, as a matter of fact," replied Charles.

"And... you think he has a particular interest in Deirdre?" prodded Lady Penrose.

"Hasn't that been obvious?" It was Ellerby's turn to look surprised. "Why, today he implied that the matter would be settled by tonight. I assumed by that he means to make his offer at the ball, though why he waited so long I can't fathom."

The conversation broke off at that point, as the other dinner guests began to arrive. Lady Penrose's spirits, which had risen considerably at Lord Ellerby's disclosures, fell again when Lord Wrotham, who had also been invited to dinner, failed to appear. She had quite begun to count on him for help in locating her missing daughter.

The Heathertons were among those select twenty or so who made up the table, along with the Thumbles and Jamesons, of course. Julia Heatherton looked round eagerly for Deirdre, claiming to have a new bit of gossip she wished to impart, but she was not in the drawing-room, where the party was assembled.

When she could delay no longer, Lady Penrose led them into the dining room on the arm of Lord Ellerby. At this point, Miss Heatherton could not restrain her curiosity.

"But where is Didi, Lady Penrose?" she asked in her high, carrying voice. "She is not ill, I hope? And I was certain she told me that Lord Wrotham was to be present tonight, as well!" Her rather long nose twitched, as if scenting a scandal.

The Baroness looked regally around the table as all eyes

turned towards her for her answer. "Oh, did I not tell you? The announcement was to be made during the ball, in any case. Deirdre and Lord Wrotham are betrothed, and he has taken her to meet his great-aunt. I hope they shall return by suppertime, but the great-aunt is an eccentric creature and may well insist that they stay the night." She maintained a serene expression, giving no hint of the fact that she had invented the entire story, not to mention Lord Wrotham's great-aunt, even as she spoke.

Celeste turned a startled face towards her mother and no doubt would have spoken had Charles not touched her arm and gently shaken his head. "It will do vastly more harm than good to contradict her, you know," he cautioned her in a whisper. The excited murmur which had broken out at the Baroness's words ensured that no one else overheard.

"Oh, but..." Her thoughts finally catching up with her mouth, Celeste subsided.

Beata and Althea were among the most amazed at this unexpected intelligence. Beata regarded her mother suspiciously, as though fearing that all was not quite as it seemed, but she was wise enough to hold her tongue for the present. Althea was less restrained.

"But why did you not tell us last night, Mama?" she demanded. "And why was Lord Wrotham not there at the rout with Didi?"

Lady Penrose regarded her eldest daughter with less than her usual fondness. "It was not settled till this morning," she lied calmly. "And Lord Wrotham had another engagement last night. But," she said brightly, changing the subject, "I apprehend that one or two of you are not aware of the other betrothal in our family. My dear Celeste is promised to Lord Ellerby here. That also is to be announced tonight."

This successfully turned the conversation, much to Lady Penrose's relief. She had never been especially creative, and feared that her story would quickly crumble were it too diligently questioned.

As the dinner party broke up to proceed to the ballroom, Beata took the opportunity to draw her mother to one side. "Mama, what fustian is this?" she demanded in a fierce whisper. "I know very well that Deirdre was missing late this afternoon, for Peters came by to see if I knew where she might be. Do I take it that she has not yet returned?"

Lady Penrose very nearly broke down at this, but drew on her years of breeding to contain her emotions. "No, Beata," she confessed quietly, "she has not. I am at my wits' end wondering what can have happened to her."

"I was afraid of that. Mama, I had no chance to tell you before dinner, but just as I was leaving my house one of my footmen told me that Deirdre had been seen this afternoon climbing into a coach with Mr. Flinder."

For a moment, Lady Penrose looked as though she might swoon. "Dear God! You do not think she has eloped with him? What will Lord Wrotham say?"

Beata shook her head. "I cannot think she went with him willingly!"

Lady Penrose said miserably, "It makes little matter. Her reputation must be ruined by now! Any marriage forced upon her can be set aside, of course, but Wrotham will scarcely want aught to do with her now." She took a deep breath, suddenly recalling that she was hostess at a ball. Her innate optimism reasserted itself. "Not a word of this to anyone!" she cautioned Beata. "All may come right in the end; one never knows."

Beata clearly thought that unlikely in the extreme, but promised to stay mum.

As the ball progressed, Lady Penrose clung to her smile as she glibly answered any questions put to her about Deirdre's absence and her supposed engagement to the much-sought-after Marquis of Wrotham. Miss Heatherton, in particular, seemed inclined to doubt the story, making the baroness wonder uncomfortably whether the girl had heard something. If anyone could be depended upon to spread a scandal, it was Julia Heatherton.

Upon reflection, Lady Penrose realized that she would have done much better to have told everyone that Deirdre was ill, or even dead, rather than to drag Lord Wrotham's name into something which might well become unsavoury. She was considering whether there were any way that she could reasonably retract her story when Peters, at her elbow, informed her that her presence was urgently required in the kitchen.

"In the kitchen?" she repeated in disbelief. This footman generally knew his business, but now it appeared that he needed some correction. "Can you not see that there is a ball taking place, of which I am the hostess? Surely the cook can handle a shortage of lobster patties, or whatever the difficulty is, on her own!"

"Please, my lady," repeated Peters, his face now betraying suppressed excitement. "It... it concerns Miss Deirdre."

All manner of visions instantly arose before the Baroness's eyes, foremost among them an apparition of her daughter's senseless body lying prostrate in the scullery. She came at once.

As Peters led her through the busy kitchen to the small

pantry behind it, her anxiety increased. The change in her expression was comical when she suddenly beheld Deirdre, apparently in perfect health but with clothes badly stained and torn, arm in arm with the Marquis of Wrotham, who was in similar state. Both were smiling.

"But... Beata said you had gone off with Mr. Flinder!" she blurted out before considering her words, so astounded was she.

Lord Wrotham's smile faded slightly. "Beata?" he asked sharply.

"My sister, Mrs. Jameson," Deirdre supplied. "We can depend upon her discretion, Ed, have no fear."

Lady Penrose nodded numbly in agreement, much distracted by hearing the Marquis called "Ed" by her daughter. They appeared to have reached some sort of understanding.

"Yes, Mother, Mr. Flinder indeed carried me off, intending to take me to Gretna Green," said Deirdre, turning her attention back to the bewildered Lady Penrose. "Lord Wrotham was obliging enough to rescue me." The look she turned upon the Marquis spoke volumes.

"You... you did not call him out, my lord?" the Baroness asked Lord Wrotham tentatively, yet another scandal rearing its ugly head in her imagination.

"No, I felt he had suffered enough already," was the enigmatic reply. "It is rather a long story, my lady, which would be better told at another time. Suffice it to say that your daughter is perfectly safe."

"Thank you, my lord," said Lady Penrose warmly. Then she remembered something else. "I... I fear in my anxiety to explain Deirdre's absence I have taken a liberty, my lord," she confessed abruptly, turning rather pink. "I have put it about that the two of you are betrothed, and that you have taken her to visit your great-aunt. Of course, you may deny it at once; I am simply glad to have my daughter home safely." She regarded him anxiously, trying to gauge his reaction.

"I think a denial will not be necessary," said Wrotham, smiling down at Deirdre. "As it happens, your daughter has already consented to become my wife. I have no great-aunt, but if I did, I have no doubt she would be pleased."

"Everything is perfectly all right, then!" exclaimed Lady Penrose, her face suddenly wreathed in smiles. "I shall write to your father first thing tomorrow, Didi!" she went on. "Surely, just this once, he will not mind if the announcement is made before his formal approval of the match."

"We would not wish to disregard the proprieties on such an important matter," said Wrotham seriously, earning a concerned look from Lady Penrose and a startled one from Deirdre. "I wouldn't dream of taking Lord Penrose's approval for granted." His eyes began to twinkle. "Therefore, it is just as well that I have already obtained his consent myself."

Simultaneously, Lady Penrose and Deirdre exclaimed, "What?"

Looking somewhat sheepish, he admitted, "Yes, that is the business which took me from Town. I wished to be very sure of you, Deirdre," he told his future marchioness with a look that checked the indignant retort on her lips.

What could she say? Deirdre was so happy at that moment that it was impossible to be the least bit angry at his high-handedness.

Lady Penrose, however, abruptly returned to the present. "Gracious!" she cried. "I had near forgotten the ball! If we are to make the formal announcement tonight, you had best run upstairs and change, miss!" she admonished her daughter. "You may use the back stairs. And you, my lord, are scarce fit for a ballroom yourself." Now that the shock was past, Lady Penrose was becoming her usual, managing self again.

Lord Wrotham looked down at his attire ruefully. "Quite true, my lady," he agreed. "I shall hurry home to change and return as soon as possible." He looked at Deirdre to find her still regarding him dreamily.

"Are you with us, my dear?" he asked gently, in sudden concern that she might not yet have completely recovered from the various shocks of the day.

Deirdre started, blinking up at him. "I have only just recalled the poem I composed while riding upside-down with that highwayman," she explained. "The ending will make it quite an epic, I vow. I must write it down immediately!"

"Deirdre," said her mother severely. "You shall do no such thing. Lord Wrotham will not wish his marchioness to become known as a bluestocking poet! You will have to put such things behind you and learn to behave as will befit your new station in life."

Deirdre glanced uncertainly at the Marquis, who smiled broadly at her before turning to Lady Penrose.

"I fear I must disagree, my lady," he retorted smoothly. "A poet of such promise as your daughter must not hide her light under a bushel. Nor would I ever ask her to neglect something of such importance to her."

Deirdre gasped with delight, but Lady Penrose looked nonplussed. "Well, of course, if you wish it, my lord," she said vaguely. Then, "Dear me! I must return to my guests at once! I told Beata everything would come right. How surprised she will be!" So saying, she bustled out of the pantry, leaving Deirdre and Lord Wrotham alone.

Deirdre turned her rapturous gaze on the Marquis. "Did you truly mean it?" she breathed. "I may compose whenever I wish?"

Wrotham turned a glance of utmost tenderness on her. "When we are wed, I shall expect your poetry to take a very prominent place in our lives, second only to my love for you."

Taking her in his arms, he began to demonstrate the extent of that love.

~

Keep reading for a preview of *Lord Dearborn's Destiny*, Hiatt Regency Classics #3!

LORD DEARBORN'S DESTINY
(PREVIEW)

"Won't you at least consider it, Forrest? As a favour to me?" The Countess of Dearborn cocked her head at her son in a manner intended to be winsome, but which made her enormous purple turban tip dangerously to one side.

"Don't tell me you would actually believe anything this Madame Fortunata might say, Mother," he replied with a snort, one golden brow sceptically arched. "I can assure you that I won't."

"Then you'll come?" Lady Dearborn was ecstatic. "I promise you won't regret it. Fortunata isn't Cora's real name, of course; I knew her when she was plain Mrs. Lawrence, back when she did readings only for a few friends, but now she is become ever so popular. Having one's fortune told is all the thing these days, you know."

"So is pink embroidery on one's waistcoat, I have heard, but you'll notice that my own singularly lacks it."

"Now, Forrest, don't tease," said the Countess, rising with a

213

flutter of feathers and scarves to lay a tiny beringed hand on her son's sleeve. "You know how much this means to me."

He did. For as long as Forrest could remember, Lady Dearborn had relied heavily on superstition, folk tales and charms to order her daily life. As a child, he had been forced to eat gooseberries, which he detested, every Whit Sunday as well as pancakes, which he liked rather better, on Shrove Tuesday. And he could still vividly recall, at a distance of some twenty years, his mother's hysteria over a maid's broken looking-glass, presaging ill luck for the entire household. The fact that her worst fears were never realized had no apparent effect on her blind faith in such omens.

"I will come, Mother. But I warn you—" his eyes narrowed "—do not expect me to do anything foolish, no matter how many offspring your Gypsy foretells for me. *If* I marry, 'twill be to someone of my own choosing and in my own time."

"Certainly, Forrest, certainly!" agreed Lady Dearborn in shocked accents. "I would never presume to make such a decision for you."

The Earl of Dearborn smiled in spite of himself. "No, only to nudge me in the proper direction. Do you really want grandchildren so desperately as all that?"

"I'll not say another word on the subject," declared the Countess, her chin in the air. "Cora's predictions must speak for themselves." She rang for her abigail, a middle-aged woman as stolid and sensible as her mistress was flamboyant and eccentric. "My amethyst cloak, Marie, and the lilac-and-silver scarf."

Marie extracted the required items from a wardrobe overflowing with feathers, scarves and gauzes of every hue, with shades of purple and red predominating. A sleek Siamese cat batted at the scarf as it wafted past, but Marie, with deftness born of long practice, whisked it up out of reach of the playful sable paw.

Well wrapped against the early April chill, Lady Dearborn paused long enough to tuck a curled silver feather into her turban. Nodding at her reflection in the dressing-table mirror, she turned to her son and pronounced herself ready to leave.

"I trust Madame Fortunata will not be long-winded with her prognostications," observed the Earl as they descended to his waiting curricle. "I am expected for nuncheon at White's before one."

∼

Following his mother's directions, Lord Dearborn was surprised when she told him to rein in his pair before a perfectly respectable-looking Town house of ample proportions on Brook Street.

"Your Madame Fortunata lives here?" he asked incredulously. "She must do exceedingly well gulling the ton out of their money."

"Cora is only Madame Fortunata on Tuesday and Thursday mornings," the Countess explained. "The rest of the time she is Mrs. Lawrence, as I said before, and quite well received. I daresay you have met her at some of the dos yourself."

"Indeed" was the Earl's only comment. Leaving his groom to walk the horses to prevent their becoming chilled, he escorted his mother up the broad front stairs where a butler, looking much like any other butler in London, admitted them to the house.

"Sylvia, my dear!" Rising to meet them as they entered a

parlour that was in no way out of the ordinary was a short, matronly woman, dressed far more conservatively than the Countess. "You induced him to come, I see." Turning to the Earl, she said cryptically, "Your mother has warned me that you are a sceptic, my lord, so I thought it best that we meet first in here."

"I am charmed to make your acquaintance, Mrs. Lawrence —or is it Madame Fortunata today? It is Thursday, is it not?"

Their hostess gave a long, tinkling laugh. "A sceptic indeed, I see! It is only in my astrological sanctum that I become Madame Fortunata, my lord, while in any other part of the house I remain plain Cora Lawrence." She waved him to a chair, seating herself across from him. "Will you have a cup of tea, or would you prefer that we begin forthwith?" Her question was directed at the Earl, but she glanced at Lady Dearborn for guidance as she spoke.

"Forrest did say something about another engagement—" the Countess began.

"Yes, yes, let us get the mumbo jumbo over with," said the Earl quickly. "I've no doubt my mother has told you to predict eight or ten brats for me over the next dozen years. Not that I intend to comply." He glanced sidelong at the Countess, who feigned great interest in the gilded moulding of the mantelpiece. "Where is this astrology room of yours?"

Mrs. Lawrence appeared more amused than offended at his manner. "Very well, my lord, I see we must waste as little of your precious time as possible. This way, if you please." Rising smoothly, she led the way out of the parlour and across the front hall to a door at the base of the curving staircase.

Watching Mrs. Lawrence walking ahead of them in her

fashionable pearl-grey, high-necked morning gown, Forrest found it difficult to reconcile her unremarkable appearance with his mother's stories of her uncanny ability as a fortune-teller. Cora Lawrence looked like any of a dozen other Society matrons he had met at various respectable gatherings.

"Wait here a moment," she said before disappearing behind a plain, oak-panelled door. No more than a minute later, she called out from within, "You may enter now."

Without hesitation, the Earl turned the knob and pushed open the door, only to stand mesmerized on the threshold. The room, apparently windowless, was lit by a single candle on a small table at its centre. Cloth of midnight blue, spangled with silver stars, draped both the walls and the table, where their hostess was seated. She herself was startlingly transformed by a voluminous robe and turban of the same material. Spread out before her on the table was a large sheet of parchment, curling at the edges as though very old. Beside it was a globe of crystal, mounted on an ornate bronze stand.

"Go on," whispered the Countess from behind him.

Forrest blinked once, then proceeded into the room. "Am I to sit here, ma'am?" he asked blandly as his composure returned, gesturing at the only other chair.

Mrs. Lawrence —or Madame Fortunata now, he supposed — inclined her head regally, and he seated himself across from her. The parchment, he saw, was a chart of the constellations. He had read a fair amount of astronomy at Oxford, but had no idea what the various notations around the stars meant. Something to do with his future, no doubt, he thought cynically.

As if in answer, Madame Fortunata pointed at a group of stars near the top edge of the chart. "This is Taurus, the sign under which you were born," she intoned in a voice markedly different from the one she had used in the parlour. "At the hour of your birth, Venus was in ascendancy and it is she whom we must consult to learn the identity of your soul mate."

"Soul mate?" he echoed incredulously.

"Sshh!" admonished Lady Dearborn from just inside the closed door.

The fortune-teller made no sign that she had heard either of them, but positioned the crystal globe over the parchment and gazed raptly into it. "I see her now. She is tall for a woman, and sculpted like the goddess herself. Hair of gold and eyes as blue as the sky."

Madame Fortunata now had Forrest's full attention. "Hair of gold, you say? Always did fancy blondes. Anything else?"

"Quiet and composed, graceful and demure. A vision of loveliness, soon to come to London for the first time. The stars can tell me no more."

"Her name, for instance?" asked Forrest. His scepticism, momentarily shaken, returned in full force. "No doubt there will be quite a few golden-haired, blue eyed debutantes this Season. How am I to know which one is my 'soul mate'?"

Madame Fortunata looked him full in the eyes. "You will know," she said.

"Come, Forrest," broke in the Countess. "Did you not say you were expected at White's? Be a dear and send your curricle back for me once you arrive. I wish to stay a bit longer and have my own horoscope read."

The Earl started, then turned, having briefly forgotten his mother's presence. "Certainly. I assume we may consider this matter closed?" At her innocent nod, he bowed to both ladies and took his leave.

"You did beautifully, Cora," said Lady Dearborn after the door had closed behind him. "I don't think he suspected a thing."

"I'm glad I was able to find that old crystal. I couldn't think of any other way to manufacture the description you suggested. Are you certain there will be a girl to fit it?" asked Mrs. Lawrence, removing her robe and turban. "I must admit you were right about the golden hair; it certainly made him prick up his ears."

"Dear Forrest has always preferred his, ah, ladies fair, though I doubt he knows that I know it," said the Countess with a chuckle. "And never fear, I've not known a Season yet without its share of blond debutantes, by nature or artifice. Trust me to discover which one has the best pedigree and pitch her at him, reminding him all the while of his destiny. Do the stars really predict him to marry this year?"

Mrs. Lawrence frowned at her chart, holding it closer to the candle. "Very possibly," she admitted. "The constellations predict a Season of surprises for your son, with an emphasis on romance."

"Well, another opera dancer would scarcely be a surprise, so I will assume that means marriage," decided Lady Dearborn with a bob of her turban. "The stars have never steered me wrong yet."

❧

Between afternoons at Gentleman Jackson's or the War Office

and evenings at cards or the theatre, Lord Dearborn quickly forgot his amusing interlude with Madame Fortunata. He might have shared it with his friends, as a jest that they would undoubtedly enjoy, had he not felt that in relating it he would be opening his mother to their ridicule, as well. Therefore, he did not mention it to anyone, and the matter soon slipped from his mind.

One evening nearly a month later, however, as the Season was just beginning to burst upon London, the incident was recalled vividly to his memory. He was escorting his mother (who had kept her promise in not referring again to his deplorable lack of wife and heirs) to a musicale at Lady Brookhaven's when they encountered Mrs. Lawrence. Dressed as she was in a subdued, tasteful evening gown of cream silk, he could not at once remember where he had met the lady before.

"Cora! I am delighted to see you here!" exclaimed the Countess, rectifying the lapse in his memory.

"My lady," responded Mrs. Lawrence much more properly, though her smile was as warm as her friend's. "You are looking extremely well."

"Let us sit over here, out of the way, and have a nice cose," suggested Lady Dearborn, taking Mrs. Lawrence's arm. "You will excuse us, of course, Forrest."

The Earl nodded, bowing to both ladies before leaving them to their conversation. He walked thoughtfully towards the supper-room, where a lavish buffet was laid out. Seeing Mrs. Lawrence had vividly recalled her predictions to his mind, and he considered them again with a smile.

It was almost a shame, he thought, that her fortune-telling

nonsense could not actually order the future. A woman such as she had described —tall, fair, quiet and demure —would be exactly what he might look for in a wife. He had always preferred blondes, something Mrs. Lawrence could not have known, as he was careful to keep his various *affaires* from his mother's ears. As he himself topped six feet, a tall woman would complement him well, he thought. Quiet —yes, he would infinitely prefer that to the mindless chatter most schoolroom misses subjected one to. And demure —a wife who would not be constantly hanging on his sleeve, making endless demands on his attention and purse-strings. Such a female might easily tempt him into parson's mousetrap, he mused.

Unconsciously, Forrest sighed with regret as he allowed the pleasant fantasy to disperse. At thirty, a prime catch since assuming his title at eighteen, he had endured more Seasons, more fluttering debutantes and more matchmaking mamas than he cared to remember. None had come even close to that ideal. Surely it was the sheerest folly to think that just because some fortune-teller had said what she thought he wanted to hear, such a one would magically appear this Season.

Pausing at the door to the supper-room, he shook his head to clear it of such unaccustomed thoughts. It was high time he found another mistress, he decided. He had broken things off with Glorianna nearly a month ago, and had yet to find a replacement for her. Unfulfilled physical desires must surely be the reason for his wayward imagination.

He sighed again. The truth was, he was growing tired of such transient arrangements; he was lonely, in a way no mistress could remedy. *Soul mate.* Madame Fortunata's words came back to him. There was something strangely attractive in the idea of a woman, one perfect woman, intended solely for him. One who would fill the empty spaces in his life as he would fill those in hers.

Folly! he told himself firmly, putting the idea forcibly from his mind. Forrest gazed around the sumptuously furnished room, diverting his thoughts by inventing fictitious histories for those members of the gathering that he had not yet met. There, consuming lobster patties with relish, was a very young buck who doubtless considered himself a sporting gent, judging by his spotted Belcher neckcloth and the careless set of his coat. The Earl smiled to himself, imagining that scrawny figure stripped down at a boxing parlour, looking like a plucked chicken.

His glance travelled across various and sundry newcomers to the social scene, pausing occasionally on a particularly eccentric specimen. The family just entering the room did not fall into that category at first glance: father, sober and respectably clad; mother, a few years younger, handsome in an overstated way; two daughters, one small and dark, not in his style at all, whose dress was at least two years out of mode, and the other... Forrest's gaze sharpened abruptly. Tall, golden-haired and lovely, the other girl definitely merited further study.

Advancing carefully towards this vision, the Earl made closer observations. The blonde stood perfectly still, her head at a regal angle. Leaning down, she whispered something to the dark girl, who seemed to have a great deal to say in reply. While she spoke, the lady who had captured his attention merely smiled, nodding once or twice. As the group moved into the room, he was struck by the grace of her stride.

His head in a whirl at this sudden materialization of his fanciful daydream, Forrest approached to seek an introduction to the woman who was clearly his Destiny.

∼

Order _Lord Dearborn's Destiny_ now to keep reading!

AUTHOR'S NOTE

The Cygnet, first published as *The Ugly Duckling*, was my second published novel, after *Gabriella*. All of my Regency-set books take place in this same "world," with a few of the same (fictional) peripheral characters and places. Of course, for the real historic places and people, I did my best to stay true to the known facts. While each of my books stands alone, complete in itself, some readers prefer to read them in order. My traditional Regencies romances, in order, are listed in the front of this book. For all of these reissues, I have taken the opportunity to clean up a few small errors of fact and proofing, and am delighted to again share my stories with you in this new format.

~

If you enjoyed *The Cygnet*, I hope you will consider leaving a review wherever you buy or talk about books to let other like-minded readers know they might enjoy it, too.

ABOUT THE AUTHOR

Brenda Hiatt is the New York Times and USA Today best-selling author of twenty-two novels (so far), including historical romance, traditional Regency romance, time travel romance, young adult romance, and humorous mystery. In addition to writing, Brenda is passionate about embracing life to the fullest, to include scuba diving (she has over 60 dives to her credit), Taekwondo (where she recently attained her 3rd degree black belt), hiking, traveling…and reading, of course!

For a free Regency short story and the earliest news about Brenda Hiatt's books, subscribe to her newsletter at:

brendahiatt.com/subscribe

Made in the USA
Middletown, DE
28 February 2021